FIRES OF LONDON

FIRES OF LONDON

JANICE LAW

A MYSTERIOUSPRESS.COM BOOK

INTEGRATED MEDIA
NEW YORK

To Jerry

Francis Bacon was a major twentieth-century British painter. He really did live with his old nanny and his ultra-respectable lover, and he did paint in Millais's old studio. Some of his acquaintances make cameo appearances in this novel, and I have endeavored to be faithful to their personalities as well as to Bacon's life and character. However, Bacon's adventures with corpses, criminals, and cops are purely imaginary, and any resemblance there to persons living or dead is truly coincidental.

CHAPTER ONE

"Got a light?" I asked the bulky man silhouetted against the gray night sky and the faint glimmer of the Serpentine. His hand in his pocket, scritch of a match, then blue light fractured and illuminated blunt features, small dark eyes, a heavy brow ridge, and a certain brutality of expression that sent my heart pumping with the frisson of danger: better than I'd hoped. "Thanks." Darkness again. I took a quick drag of the cigarette, risking my asthmatic lungs for courtesy. "Nice night."

"Hard to see where you're bloody going. You need eyes like a cat."

"I'm surprised you don't carry a torch." Really I wasn't. Darkness was the attraction; the blackout with all its dangers and inconveniences had opened possibilities for night fliers like yours truly and this stranger.

"Well, there are always folk about, aren't there? Lights enough if you keep your eyes open."

Something I always do. The dark shape of him, losing detail but distinct against the sky, would be hard to capture but infinitely suggestive. "These warm nights one wants to be out nonetheless."

"Nonetheless," came his echo. So we were in harmony. Playing with what chords was the only question. "It's been a perfect summer."

"Perfect." Glorious weather on the edge of invasion, poison-gas attacks, and who knew what other terrors and disasters? An atmosphere I found exhilarating. "We might walk?"

He was agreeable. The splendid park trees loomed only yards away, and I smiled at the simplicity of it, not even the price of a drink between us. I smelled raw earth from the lawns and flower beds, potholed now for gun emplacements and trenches, trampled by military boots; the strong tobacco scent of my companion, who had something vaguely northern in his speech, a geography confirmed by a hint of coarse wool as the moist night dampened his tweed jacket. His voice was hoarse with pleasure and my body alive to everything and anything, the blood pounding in my ears, the tree bark rough against my hands, our frantic bodies.

I stood up, a moment to get a breath, then straightened my clothes. I started to say "We might meet again" when something stopped me. I like the rush of violence and frenzy, I do, but I've also developed a sense of self-preservation. Something whispered in my inner ear, Don't talk to him. Leave.

He was a dark and silent shape against the sky. When I moved to step away, he grabbed me by the throat.

"You'll say nothing," he said, and slammed my head back against the tree, once, twice, before leaning close to me. I could feel his breath and saliva on my face and sensed the darkness in his eyes—all exciting but unwise. "You never saw me, you don't know me. This never happened, you little bugger."

I put my hand on his wrist. "Suit yourself, mate." Voice calm; it never does to betray fear.

A beat, a hesitation, then he drew back, the hysterical anger replaced by something else, a sort of stupor. He did not move as I stepped away, and when, well down the path, I turned and looked, he was still a motionless darkness under the trees.

Afterward, I stopped by a pub, pushing through the blackout curtains to the yellow light, the bluish smoke, the possibility of some nightcap adventure. Excess is sometimes just my ticket, but I'd chosen poorly: A few fellows in uniform and several pale-faced boys on the lookout for trade—too young for me and doubtless with neither the cash nor the taste for Champagne.

So I ordered up solitude and consoled myself with weak beer, since my nan and I were on our uppers. I was enslaved to the switchboard of a third-rate London club, the habitat of dedicated swimmers who didn't pay enough to keep me in paints, never mind Champagne or Nan's chocs or the oysters we both enjoyed. Bangers and mash or baked beans had become our entrées of necessity, and Nan had pinched the last recognizable meat that graced our table. That's how she phrased it: *graced our table.* Her former profession required a genteel turn of phrase that can conceal her realism, a quality I've appreciated since infancy. Oh, I was lucky in my nanny, for as long as my manners did her credit, she was willing to prepare me for the world as it is rather than as it should be—a circumstance that has saved me more than once and that shortly improved our finances.

It happened that I was having a rare evening in; to tell the truth it was pouring with rain. I was preparing to read out the crime news and the royal calendar my nan enjoys so much when I happened to run my eye down the personals column and laughed.

"I hope you're not laughing at HRH's visit to the shipyards," she said. "He's far better—far better, stutter and all—than the duke with that trollop Wallis Simpson."

"Duchess of Windsor now," I said, just to get a rise out of her.

"Duchess of Windsor my foot. I live to see her head off." My dear nan regards capital punishment with almost indecent relish.

"I don't think they're going to bring back the headsman, Nan."

"Country'd be a damn sight better off. Her with the fancy airs and graces and American on top of everything."

"Though we wouldn't have George the Sixth, if it hadn't been for her."

"You're set to be naughty," said Nan. "I can tell, whenever you turn logical. What's up your sleeve this time?"

"I better have something," I said. "Every butcher in the neighborhood's going to be wise to you."

She made a queer little sneezing "humph." "I'm half blind. If I don't see the counter, I sometimes find myself at the door. It'd be scandalous to send me to Holloway."

"I don't care to risk that. Listen, what do you think of this: '*Gentleman's companion, complete discretion assured.*'"

"Ha," said Nan. "I should think so."

"Sort of a valet, you think?"

"Sort of a bum boy, if you ask me."

"Nanny, you do surprise me."

"I had a life before I was put to raising you, you know."

I couldn't help laughing.

"What?"

"But he's advertising in the *Times*."

"For the aura of respectability. The *Times* lends a certain air, doesn't it?"

"That's true. But Nanny, what do you think? Will he get any responses?"

"Is there only the one advert?"

"No, it seems to be a going thing. I'd never noticed."

"*Gentlemanly gentleman's companion*," said Nan straightaway. "That's what you put in. You're a cultured man; a painter and decorator who speaks French like a Frog. Not that you want any truck with foreigners."

I reminded her that I had pretty much learned "the way of the world," as she liked to phrase it, as a boy on my own in Berlin and Paris.

"That was abroad," said Nan. "This is England, dear boy. Certain standards apply. See you read me all the responses. Strictly Mayfair and the City is what you want. We might stretch as far as Chelsea, but nothing suburban. Remember that. You look for gentlemen from Mayfair. Nicer manners and apt to pay up better."

You can see why I adore her. My old nanny can cut to the heart of a problem and find a practical solution. We composed an advert and within the week my career as a "gentleman's companion" was launched with a small blizzard of letters. While my nan selected the most promising, I shined my shoes, whitened my teeth, painted up just enough—"skillful as any girl," Nan always said—and set out to make our fortune. Luckily, given my tastes, the gentlemen in question weren't always such gentlemen, but thanks to Nan's insight, they all had cash. I even attracted an art lover, a real find, and with his support we managed a certain level of comfort—Chablis if not Champagne—and recognizable meat and boxes of chocolates for Nan and decent canvas and paints for me. Soon we were set, despite the blackout, the Phony War, rationing, and the ever-present possibility of arrest and prosecution to survive very nicely. Such felicity was too good to last. "Call no man fortunate until he is dead," said the Greeks. They knew the score.

That's the reason I read the Greeks, especially Aeschylus. I'd like to paint *à la Grec*, too—not classical faces and beaux arts torsos, but the fatalism, violence, and endurance of the ancients. Have I mentioned I'm ambitious? Oh, yes. Picasso showed the way with the distortion of his Dinard paintings, those figures writhing under the pressure of their own desires—and don't I know about that! Nothing but distortion can convey the mad absurdity of contemporary life, an absurdity that was soon to be unmistakably confirmed for me. But at that precise moment, living with Nan and supported by Arnold—he's the art lover, crazy about me and about my paintings, too—I was personally as content as I'm likely to be.

For one thing, I'd acquired a new passion—no, not Arnold, though I was fond of him, very fond, and Nan found him congenial, and we both liked his company. He was comfortable, reassuring, and solvent, but for passion, I need a touch of risk and torment such as painting provides and which, thanks to Arnold, I discovered roulette does too.

Soon he had me conversant with *le rouge* and *le noir*, with placing bets *en plein* or choosing to take a flutter with *carré, cheval,* or *traversale.* I took to the wheel wholeheartedly, and it was to keep in gambling funds that we embarked on a little roulette operation of our own. Strictly illegal, *naturellement*, with the possibility of disgrace, imprisonment, and other disasters adding a fillip to the excitement.

Arnold acquired a wheel, and I constructed a table with a painted surface where the punters could place their bets. We ordered cases of Champagne and brushed our suits. Arnold spread the word discretely and hired a few wide boys of our acquaintance to serve as lookouts. We kitted them up as housepainters and set them along the block. Soon the streets around the studio were crawling with limousines. Even the big studio I was renting was barely large enough for the crush, while my dear nan debuted as hat-check girl, keeper of the WC key, and collector of tips.

Oh, we had fine times, and the house made a tidy profit. We'd end our sessions with dawn coming, the three of us sitting on the studio's moth-eaten velvet armchairs, drinking the last of the Champagne amid the litter of dirty glasses and cigarette butts, the piles of money and chips. Danger, chance, Champagne—all the necessities of life satisfactorily supplied!

And artistically? How was I doing there? Middling, dear heart. Wild ambition, mad joy, and bitter despair accompanied by the sound of tearing canvas. If something's really bad, there's nothing for it but to slice it up. If there's the faintest possibility of development, of happy accidents and sudden inspiration, scrape and paint over, but a truly unsatisfactory image will seep through to deaden any new work. Besides, destruction is the twin of creation. Rip, slash, "Off with her head," as Nanny says. I want to paint blood and flesh. I want to wake people up—even sleepy, alcoholic clubmen—and *make them look.*

At what? There's the chief thing: finding the right image. Something was coming; I could feel an idea in the back of my mind, growing but not quite full blown, so I was looking at everything and searching to find a design that would create the right effect. I was painting a lot of mouths with shiny white teeth, like the screaming woman in Poussin's *Massacre of the Innocents*, last seen when I was a boy in Paris. I wanted to paint a scream and I needed a carcass for the mouth.

I tried painting the nurse in *The Battleship Potemkin.* Have you seen that tremendous Russian film? The pure genius of Eisenstein's Odessa Steps sequence? The crowd fired upon, the nurse hit, her baby's carriage rocketing off down the steps? Emblematic of my own fate, I suspect, if not for my nan, who kept a firm hand on my young life and protected me from my mother's indifference and my father's violence.

Still, that scream moves me, and I have to find the right image for the cry of creation and destruction, of pain and pleasure, because I believe in nothing else. I'm a connoisseur of extremity, of excess emotion and extraordinary sensation, and that spring was as good a time as there ever was to indulge, what with the dodgy show in France and the suspicion that this time the Channel might not be wide enough.

I'd better tell you about one night in particular—not nearly as intense as some, but important in the larger picture. That's often the way: a little patch of color, a single line, the toning up or down of a hue can affect the whole image, so an incident that seems peripheral at the time turns out to alter your life. I was out on my own because Arnold was back for an evening with the family that he was shortly to abandon for me, for disgrace and ecstasy. It's not vanity if I say I understood his choice. Arnold was drawn to extremes, but, being respectable, personal disaster was a good deal easier and quicker to come by for him than for me.

Anyway, on the night in question—another favorite, quasi-official phrase of my nan's—I was doing my rounds, tin hat on, gas mask shouldered—I haven't mentioned yet that I was on His Majesty's Service in a modest way as an ARP warden. A certain irony in my being equipped with a badge and authority, but, as the catch phrase went, there was a war on. To my considerable relief, the military rejected asthmatics, the fire service too, so I was in Air Raid Precautions, a certified busybody who went around to check that window blinds were down and never a light showing; that car lights were off or properly shielded, torches ditto; and that pubs hid all merriment with lightproof curtains and that everyone was equipped with a gas mask.

I was laboring on the preparedness front line though there was still nary a plane in the sky or a puff of gas on the breeze. While awaiting Herr Hitler's shock troops and paratroopers, we wardens practiced for catastrophe on poor smashed pedestrians and cyclists caught broadside by darkened cars and invisible lorries, and on hellish motor accidents that began with the sudden roar of metals simultaneously meeting and ripping apart and continued in the flare of burning petrol as mangled bodies were lifted onto the sidewalk. A rehearsal, that, for horrors to come, though we didn't know it then.

My post was near the two rooms plus studio that Nan and I rented. Every evening, I checked my blocks of houses, looked in at the pubs, and reported to HQ. If all was quiet and good when my shift ended, I was free to saunter down to one of the drinking clubs that catered to gentlemen too impatient to respond to adverts or to other types who never pick up the *Times*. Not being a domestic animal, I needed a night out now and again.

When, truly, the world could be beautiful. Streets empty, sky like discolored pewter, lightening toward the Thames. A monochrome world of sound, not color. Listen for the wind, for the hum of tires on pavement, the whirr of a coasting bicycle, for footsteps, a voice. On certain narrow streets, dark as closets, I listened to my own footsteps, one hand out for pillar boxes and lampposts, or to brace my fall if a high curb surprised me. But if the moon rose out of the clouds, it was lovely, the dross and awkwardness, the architectural errors and compromises all submerged in a close harmony of silvers, blacks, and grays, and I could have walked all night but for want of a drink.

And hark, music sliding from behind thick blackout curtains issued an invitation. A half block away, down a set of basement steps, I entered a little private club favored by "resting" actors, bent coppers, and middle-aged steamers, with a side room where painted boys danced together, tangos by preference. It was a dusty, squalid place, one of a number I know, but I like contrasts; they get the blood going and I can't live without them. I like the cold, pure city of moonlight and the smoky fug of basement rooms. I like luxury and a few grand relatives, and I like squalor and hungry boys and rough trade.

I made my way into the club that night and put my tin hat on the bar to a good deal of joshing and whistling—they're all mad for uniforms—until I pulled up my pant leg to flash my fishnet stockings. This promoted such laugher that the barman, red-faced with curly black hair and a drinker's discolored nose, offered a glass of champers gratis for "cheering them up."

"Such a moaning tonight," he said. "You wouldn't believe."

"Bad night? Darlings, a warm, moonlit night in the blackout?"

"You hadn't heard, then?" A little pause. I shook my head. "Damien's bought it."

"Damien? The skinny blonde with the violet eye shadow? That Damien?" We'd had a drink together not three nights before. Not my type, but I hate to drink alone and I believe in helping the needy with the needful.

"Found him this morning—yesterday morning, I'd better say now."

"No! Had he—" First thought, of course. A slight, underfed boy with slim legs and a consumptive cough, Damien sometimes slept rough in the park. He had blue circles under his eyes from his illness and often a fine set of bruises from his livelihood.

"Someone did for him. Beat his head in."

"Some cheap thug." Opinion courtesy of a hollow-cheeked punter in a gaudy striped jacket and elaborately made-up eyes.

"Killed for a few shillings?" Possible. We all knew Damien was on the game. And fair game for any predator: timid as a mouse, the boy couldn't have weighed eight stone.

"Why else?" An ill-chosen greenish paint gave striped jacket lizard eyes.

Let me count the ways! I was about to say, then stopped. Too much knowledge can get you into trouble. I'm rarely discreet, but a man at the far end of the bar gave off a distinct whiff of cop—and of something else, more elusive, that slipped away as soon as it surfaced. "Some madman," I said.

"You're right there. You're right there!"

"Now, don't you start again, Connie. Don't start," the barman appealed.

Connie, a short youth with bad teeth and garnet lipstick, ignored this plea. "He was me mate," he wailed. "If I got down, he cheered me up. He'd have given me his last mascara."

Laughter at this, but not unkind.

"You knew him," he said to me, and I nodded. I'd painted him, as a matter of fact, a little sketch of him and Connie sitting on the sofa in my studio. A couple of years ago, that was. "You knew the sort he was. No trouble to anybody. Harmless as they come. He wouldn't have hurt anyone." He gripped my arm and began sobbing against my uniform.

"What about a drink to Damien's memory, eh?" I gestured to the barman with my glass.

"He did so like Champagne," Connie conceded, wiping his nose on his sleeve.

"Someone promise him Champagne, you think?" I asked.

"So he said. He said this one was gold. He should have taken me with him." A touch of resentment. "More fun. Safer, too."

"But not necessarily better," I suggested. Particularly for dark-hearted folk. You get them in all cities—countryside, too, no doubt, but I avoid the pastoral like the plague. I'm drawn, myself, to a certain darkness of soul, but unlike poor Damien I'm tough. I managed London on my own at sixteen and Berlin, *auf Deutsch* no less, picked up gratis from a lot of elderly steamers. I did even better in Paris, my finishing school, where I had contacts and fluent French and developed an eye for the main chance. Of necessity, I've been a quick study. I was expelled on suspicion of immorality after two years in a minor public school, and I've learned most of what's been useful to me, including furniture design and the rudiments of oil painting, from randy middle-aged men with an eye for youthful faces. Bless them all—or ninety percent of them anyway. Still, bad thoughts about Damien and bodies in the street. I paid for the round and left.

"Mind yourself in the dark," said the barman.

I slapped on my tin hat and tapped it. "Off on His Majesty's service," I said. His laughter followed me, and I turned and waved to him at the curtain. The heavy type at the end had raised his head. Copper? I was sure of it now.

CHAPTER TWO

Nan was in the kitchen with her wireless on, a birthday gift from me with a little help from Arnold, who finds her amusing. She was listening to the evacuation news on the Beeb. A bloody disaster. Belgium finished, French lines collapsed, armies streaming for the coast and Dunkirk. I'm not best suited for regimentation, and living with my father inoculated me against all the temptations of brass and polish. I'm not even fond of guardsmen, that traditional London recreation, but boys I know are in France, and with better lungs I could be stranded on the beach myself. Lately, what with car crashes and pedestrian disasters, I've seen blood and dismemberment on a small scale, and I can imagine worse. I don't like the picture.

The news reader was giving out the surprisingly high evacuation numbers—more than 100,000 already—and describing the small boats crossing the channel to help, but from my studio I was watching a crisis nearer to home. Nan was preparing some carrots, and I noticed that she filled the pot by ear, tipping her head to listen to the rising sound of the water. She selected the carrots by touch, which made me unhappy about the paring knife, even though she's skillful. Slow but skillful.

I'd stepped back for a moment to check the proportions on my canvas when I realized that I could see her feeling for the thin root end of each carrot, checking that she'd cut all the leaves, and listening for the water. She sometimes jokes about her eyes—"I've no more sight than a bat," she'll say. Then she sets off for the shops and lifts something if we're short though she's nearly blind. Admit it; Nan's nearly blind. She must judge the clerk's presence by sound—an appalling, exciting risk, such as I appreciate, but still . . . at her age. That's another topic I normally avoid, because, although normally fearless, I'm fearful for Nan, whom I love. I'm quite aware that she's all that stands between me and total self-absorption. And beyond that, what would I do without her in so many practical ways?

"Need some help, Nan?"

"No, but come hear this, dear boy. We're getting them home! Frenchies, too. Herr Hitler doesn't know who he's dealing with this time."

I stuck my brushes in a jar of turps and wiped my hands.

"If only the weather holds. It's got to hold another day or so."

"How many left?"

"Three, four hundred thousand."

I shook my head. Ypres numbers, Paschendale numbers—the hitherto unimaginable dimensions of the last war.

"We'll get them," said Nan. "We'll get them. The British Navy's worth more than all those damn panzers. You'll see."

I gave her a hug. "So, dinner, Nan. What's on tonight?" I didn't want to talk about the disaster across the Channel; I'd like to have switched off the set, but Nan was rapt. It's as if the war never really ended for her generation, as if the past twenty years has been one long truce, and they've expected this all the time.

And they were right; disaster's always waiting in the wings or down in some basement accommodation. Consider poor consumptive Damien, who lingers in my mind. I'd gotten more details by then: he'd been dumped in the park with his head bashed in and multiple cuts and bruises. We shared lung trouble, Damien and I; we were acquainted with suffocation, with screams inside and out. With the human condition, I'm tempted to add, for now came the report that the Jerries were strafing the beaches and ships. I was only distracted from visions of flames and blood when I noticed Nan touching the knobs on the stove. Would she attempt the burner and threaten the whole block? "Light the stove for me, dear boy," she said. One crisis averted; she knows her limitations, at least for today.

And do I know mine? A good question that may soon be answered, because I've now seen "the cop" several times since I spotted him the night I learned Damien had been murdered. He's just around, nothing aggressive—he lives in Chelsea for all I know—but he's become someone I notice leaving the newsstand, perhaps, or waiting for a bus or sitting well back in a pub. Though it's quite irrational, I think that's why the unlucky Damien sticks in my mind's eye, lying naked in the high grass of the park, disfigured and dead. Modern distortion, if you like. I've made three "Damien" paintings since but sliced them all up. Damien alone is too simple. David, remember, painted the dead Marat. And Goya—you can hardly speak of Goya without corpses and atrocities. I'm still looking for the right image for Damien and for my scream, too.

Although there, given our catastrophic historical moment, the daily press has been an inspiration. I've been cutting out pictures of Hitler and Mussolini, who wear interesting hats and want to devour the earth. I can use them. I've begun painting Hitler's limousine with its gleaming sides and little swastikas, and I want to put Damien in there too, another screamer. I'm not sure how I'm going to do that, as I have some difficulties with indicating space. I'll maybe have to get rid of the big car and turn the shape into Damien on his knees in the park, pleading for his life. You can do that with oil paints, scrape and paint over and turn one thing into another—and leave traces of the original underneath, too, if there's some relationship. If. An oil painting carries traces of its own history, a record that some days I like—and other days I destroy.

What I don't like is the cop—as yet unnamed. It may be just paranoia, but I've finally admitted to myself that some copper's got his eye on me. I'd better find out who he is and what he's up to, especially if he's drinking in the private clubs. Not the Europa, thank God; Maribelle wouldn't allow, so I'm set there. And lately I've made a point of walking about with Arnold—he's an alderman and safe as houses. Naturally, in another way, danger itself is tempting, but I must remember Oscar Wilde and jail. With my habits, I'm indictable almost any night of the week.

What do I know about my own private cop? Higher rank, I think. Too old to be a constable and no trace of a uniform. Now, there's a hope: maybe he finds guardsmen too flashy and has a yen for my ARP uniform. This I find fanciful. I'd better face it: he's on to something. Our gambling evenings are the obvious possibility, although Arnold says everyone's happy, and I've seen myself that Jack and Billy and the others watch the street like rats with cheese. Recently we got the wind up and canceled a session. After that, I didn't see my copper for a week, and I thought, Right, I'm home free. Then the other night, an unsettling incident.

I was doing my rounds: "Light showing, Mrs. Brown. Top left window"; "Light through the transom, Mr. Green"; "Blackout not adequate at all, Mrs. Simmons." Followed up with the usual excuses. Mrs. Simmons is poor, genuinely, so I said she should use her back room tonight and I'd bring 'round some of my canvas fragments and some stretchers to seal off the front windows tomorrow. She gave me a couple fingers of gin before I put my tin hat back on. Technically, I'd just been bribed to avoid a fine; practically, I'd helped a neighbor. Point of view is everything in such matters.

Anyway, I was walking along with my hooded torch and the smell of juniper berries on my breath when I heard steps behind me—a sound that's rather lost its erotic appeal since Damien, whose death did nothing to disturb the good burghers, I'm sure, but gave us not-so-good burghers a turn. Yes, indeed, even if my tastes run to older men, my own history—well, not relevant here. But steps behind me were definitely now a matter of concern as well as interest.

I turned around to shine my torch on him. I'm official, after all. I may be a poof running an illegal gambling op, but with badge and tin hat I'm on His Majesty's business and you can bet I'm conscientious. What do I see for my trouble? My cop, *naturellement*—a familiar, stoutish figure in a dark raincoat and sturdy shoes. He wore a fedora low on his broad and heavy forehead, all as usual, but now the angle of the light, low and from below, highlights the planes of his face, blunt and a tad brutal, a revelation of a personality last glimpsed by the flare of a match in the park. I got a shock, although in another instant I was doubtful. The park encounter had been several months ago, and I'd seen the man's face for a matter of seconds, though seconds is enough if you really look at something. Was he the same man I'd since marked for a cop? And would it be worse or better if he were? "Evening, Inspector," I said; it never hurts to guess higher in rank.

He stopped and looked at me but, and this was the key thing, he didn't recognize me; I'm sure he didn't, even if he was the man in the park—and I was leaning again toward the idea that he was. He might know me from the club; he sat and stared at me long enough, but not from the park, or else my tin hat's a better disguise than I'd thought. Still, he wasn't best pleased. He thought he was in deep disguise, totally civilian, as if unaware that he carries the smell of the lockup with him at all times.

"Evening, Warden. All quiet tonight?"

"Pretty much," I said. "Just waiting for Jerry."

He grunted. We've all been waiting for months, and it had gotten so that we were torn between dread of the event and a desire to end the suspense.

"You haven't a torch," I said, and, I noticed, no gas mask either.

When he didn't answer, I could tell he was wondering about me in some way.

"You've forgotten your mask, too." I fumbled my notepad open.

"A sudden call." Though he waved his hand in dismissal, he made no move and his stillness, almost amounting to torpor, made me deeply uneasy with its echoes of the park and the aftermath of violence. This was the man.

"Your name?" At the very least I had to take his name.

He cleared his throat and said, reluctantly and heavily, "Chief Inspector Mordren. John Mordren."

"Address, sir?"

He gave his substation instead of his residence, but I didn't feel able to press him. "Don't let me catch you again without your mask," I said. "We can't risk having a chief inspector gassed." Don't you think my tone was admirable?

He found his tongue then. "Glad to see you're doing your job, Warden." As if he was pleased to give me a passing grade. Like hell.

"On your way to the Underground, sir?" I gestured with my light, offering an escort—we do that sometimes to be helpful, to build the "community support" so important for us licensed pains in the ass.

He seemed to recall himself and nodded. I started toward the South Kensington stop, figuring he was headed into the City, but no, he wanted the nearer Knightsbridge stop, just a hop from the park. That suggested interesting possibilities. "Right." I took a glance at him as we walked along—he was half a head taller, maybe four stone heavier. Everything about him was weighty in all senses of the word, including the atmosphere he carried with him. What did he want? Well, I could guess the obvious, and I was half tempted to ask him for a light and see how he'd react.

"Curb coming; careful, sir." Ever the polite and helpful warden—my manners really are exemplary. A sound of tires—it's hard sometimes to judge the distance. I stopped and he did too. Then a rumble as a heavy lorry, probably military by its narrow, shielded beams, roared past, and he stepped forward to cross before, in one of those better instincts that so often bring disastrous consequences, I grabbed his arm. "Not yet. There's another one."

And there was: a dark, fast-moving car washed us with wind. I raised my torch but could not read its plate. "If Jerry doesn't hurry up, we'll all be dead beforehand."

He stared at me for a moment, and I was glad my tin hat shaded my eyes. "The angel of the lord has passed over us," he said. Which didn't strike me as normal police conversation, but admittedly we were in a peculiar situation.

"Exactly, sir, though I do sometimes wonder about the efficacy of the blackout. Given the casualties."

"Casualties in every war, Warden," he said with a change in tone, as if he'd suddenly woken up and was now really a chief inspector with serious business requiring his attention. "The stop's ahead. I'll find it from here, thank you." He crossed the street briskly and disappeared into the gloom.

My first thought was to follow him, though at this time of night the trains were few and the platforms half empty. Walk, maybe? I could probably make it to the park stop before the train. And then we'd see. I'd be late back to the ARP HQ, but it wouldn't be the first time. I could find a call box, invent an illness for Nan—I can be a shameless liar in times of need. Off the mark at top speed, sweeping my torch before me to avoid the curbs, the pavement cracks, the stray dustbin lids and bicycles that made our rounds a shin-bashing obstacle course. I was making good time when a faint light bobbed in front of me. Tin hat, uniform. "Have you got your gas mask, mate?"

"Of course. I'm a warden." I raised my torch in the hopes of dashing away, but no such luck. I knew him: Liam Silver, frizzy ginger hair, snub nose, small green eyes. Punctilious.

"What are you doing on my patch?"

Liam favored military slang and a military style, which didn't do much for our "community relations."

"Escorting a civilian to the Underground," I said. Note use of the word "civilian." The way to his heart.

"You're past the stop now."

Suspicious bastard. "What street is this? Have I gotten turned around?" How fortunate it is that people are usually willing to believe one's stupidity.

"That's your lack of military training," he said. "I can tell you that my experience in night navigation has been helpful in this job. Now, you're probably navigating by that steeple, but I have . . . blah, blah, blah . . . "

I could feel my quarry slipping away. Even on the night schedule, my cop would have gotten a train by this time and be on his way either to the park or to points unknown. I let Silver enlighten me about the streets around me and night navigation and several other topics. Why? Why make enemies is why, and that was prudent, because as we strolled back toward what he referred to as "your patch," I was able to remark that even some police were without their masks. "People are getting complacent," I said.

"Policeman? I hope you wrote him up." That's Warden Silver. A stickler for rules.

"A warning," I said. "He was called out suddenly."

"No excuse," said Silver.

"Would you know him? An Inspector Mordren. I'm wondering if he lives near here."

"Not a name I'm familiar with."

"Perhaps an emergency," I said, though I didn't believe it.

"He should still have had his mask," said Silver.

CHAPTER THREE

Through his political connections, Arnold discovered that, far from sniffing out our roulette wheel, Inspector Mordren was in the homicide division, news that cheered him more than me, although it meant that we could carry on with the casino evenings. Without entire success, I told myself that the inspector lived locally, that he was just another lover of the blackout, that my glimpses of him in the street, at The Pond, at the newsstand—even in the park—were purest coincidence, and that the anxiety of his lurking presence was just a product of the now-universal nervous strain. We were fortunate that we had gambling to distract us from the false (though ever-alarming) air-raid warnings and from the battle overhead, where the Luftwaffe and the RAF were losing planes by the score. So far, our Hurricanes and Spitfires had proved a match for the Messerschmitts and Junkers, while, in a triumph for British engineering and aviation, the feared Stuka dive-bombers had already been knocked out of the fight. But even the most sanguine civilian could calculate that our losses of men and machines must be immense. Every day planes plunged into the Channel or crash-landed in fields and suburban gardens while pilots' chutes blossomed in the high blue sky.

I found it hard to imagine aerial blood and fire—though I was getting well acquainted with both down below—or how the ground must look flattened and tiny when seen from a great height, or the terrible fall of man and machine. The nearest we got to comprehending this strange new high-altitude warfare was in the pubs, where we met the aftereffects in exhausted men, their eyes focused immensely far away, who were trying to come down from too much adrenaline and too little sleep. There were others, too, in the worn uniforms of the defeated French, Polish, Czech, and Belgian forces: worried, angry men, eager to be mobilized, eager for revenge—and all desperate for momentary pleasure. I confess I found compensations.

Overhead as constant reminders of our highly provisional safety, elephantine barrage balloons floated, silver against the summer sky, creating a curious new upper story for a city that remained basking in the sunlight, day after day. "It was a lovely summer in '14, too," said Nanny. She occupied herself with the wireless and the newspapers, which Arnold read to her almost every night while I was on my dreary ARP rounds. Everybody was bored with the blackout, fed up with rationing—recently extended to meat—weary of overfilled trains, and on tenterhooks about the battle, at once remote and ever present, that would decide our fate.

In this atmosphere of the big wager, smaller bets made perfect sense. Whenever we had money, Arnold and I went to a club and played roulette. He promised me Monte Carlo when the war was over, but I enjoyed even the smallest, seediest clubs. I liked to watch the gamblers, obsessed, exhilarated, desperate: large wins and losses reveal all the strong emotions. I liked the late hours, too, for though I rise early to paint every day, I sleep very little, and I find the nights long unless I'm drinking and gambling and out on the town.

I used to arrange to meet Arnold somewhere after my ARP rounds. I'd arrive to see him holding open the club door, a drink in one hand, a cigarette in the other; he'd have been on the lookout for me. "Dear boy, I'm going to be lucky tonight!" He always believed that; he was an optimistic gambler, even though he spun the wheel on our own casino nights and knew the odds and had taught them to me. Nonetheless, when he was on the other side of the table, he believed in winning. I found this curious but endearing, like Arnold himself—bald and not especially handsome, but the right age for me and well built with broad shoulders. He was a gentle, kindly person, which, given the perversity of desire, was both an attraction and a demerit. What one likes in daily life—courtesy, consideration, good humor—is not necessarily the soil in which one's erotic life flourishes. The pattern of mine was set early on by my powerful, drunken father—a development that was surprising to me and doubtless would have been an utter and unwelcome revelation to him. But we had little contact after I left home at sixteen.

Arnold was as unlike as possible. He was a success rather than a failure, a gentleman rather than a brute. Arnold was a husband and father, a politician, a pillar of the community and utterly respectable, but it was all, on one level, a lie. His effort to be just what he was supposed to be moved me because, except for Nan, I've never cared enough about other people to worry what they thought of me.

But Arnold thinks about others, and so he became what they wanted. His family wanted him to be "normal"—whatever that is. I don't think it exists. We're all queer one way or the other, and I think it's quite arbitrary what's the done thing in bed. His wife wanted a husband, then children, then a position in the community. What Arnold himself really wants is the golden apple, the forbidden. He wants to risk everything because if he loses, he'll be free. I understand that. Winning brings him one sort of freedom—freedom to drink Champagne and buy my paintings and purchase more chips. But losing—losing might open a whole new world. So he plays, though he knows better, and he believes in winning.

I'm an entirely different sort of gambler. I believe in loss. Wins come occasionally, of course—just the law of averages—but eventually complete loss is as certain as mortality. That's why I found the wheel exciting; one risks a sort of death with the possibility of resurrection, and that summer we grew more and more reckless, playing for the highest stakes whenever we could, recouping our inevitable losses with our own illicit casino and blocking any anxieties with Champagne.

That was nighttime in the summer of 1940; night was for sensation, for risk and ecstasy. In the morning, I had to face my canvas. I'd started doing large paintings by then, though the first thing of mine to attract notice was small: a little biomorphic crucifixion. My subject. My great ambition is to paint a major crucifixion, to find a new way into that old motif, and in its pursuit I've ripped more canvas than you can imagine. Why, when I'm not religious, certainly not Christian? Because, like roulette, the crucifixion figures forth the shape and dimension of life.

As a child in Ireland, I was taught that God sent his only begotten son to be crucified. The old Anglican priest found that a mystery, but given my father, it didn't seem strange to me at all. The old and powerful make the young and weak suffer, and the only curious thing was that Christ's misery should have been in some way for our benefit. I don't see that. A shattered Tommy dies in agony on the beach at Dunkirk; an airman plummets from the sky with his parachute in shreds; or, closer to home, an old lady I found on Kings Road has her back and both her legs broken by a lorry and bleeds to death in the darkness. Who benefits from such calamities?

Not me. I stood frozen in the drizzle, stunned for a moment by the rasping groans of the woman and the throb of the lorry that had screeched to a halt halfway down the block. I saw her umbrella, still open, perched beside her like a giant bat, and my first thought was of Nan. For an instant, I saw Nan lying in the street, blood pouring from her nose and mouth, and I thought my heart would stop, but it didn't; or if it did, it restarted at top speed. I shouted to the driver. He had a torch, and I ordered him to stand on the pavement and wave his light to warn oncoming vehicles. His face was white and young; he kept saying that we had to get her onto the sidewalk. I knew moving her would be disastrous and told him so. At the phone box I shouted my report then raced back. In part of my mind, she was still Nan, but I arrived too late for any comfort. I found her up on the sidewalk, both driver and lorry gone. Though we have our orders and procedures, sometimes there are no good choices. Within the cone of my torch lay darkness, blood, livid flesh: a crucifixion of sorts—*a very present agony*, as the old priest used to say. I must find an image to do that justice.

Which is my work for day. Work lasts until one or so, when I eat lunch with Nan and we have our daily visit—"a wee natter" as she calls it—when we discuss the Beeb reports and I read her the morning papers, the *Times* and the *Telly*. I do this quite mindlessly. For some reason, I never take in the full sense of words when I'm reading aloud, probably because I'm conscious of reading clearly and distinctly as Nan always insisted. One day I was reading out an account of a strangulation, a man who murdered his wife over burnt toast or a bad sausage or some other trifle, when I realized that Nan, who heard the crime news from two or three different papers a day, might be an untapped resource.

"Nan," I said, deciding to make a test. "Remember the case of that boy found dead in Hyde Park a little while ago?"

"Beaten to death and left naked," she said promptly. "You stick to your gentlemen." As you can see, she knew me well.

"Was there ever any more on the story?"

Nan looked at me. With her thick glasses, her eyes are enormous, like an owl's or a lemur's; if they don't see much, they're rarely fooled by what they do see. "You knew him, did you?"

"Not well. I bought him a drink once."

"He didn't look out for gentlemen," she said sharply. She was about to elaborate when I broke in.

"The *Telegraph* reports didn't have very much information. I wondered how the investigation was going."

Nanny thought for a moment. "All quiet there," she said, "though it's a terrible business. But with no certain address and no relatives, the police won't strain themselves."

I agreed that was likely. "Would you remember the investigating officer? The name?"

"No one mentioned," she said. "Maybe if they a get a lead, but everything depends on the battle, of course." That was the first time Nan had given even the faintest indication she thought things might go badly. "Not that we won't give them what-for if they try to land. You let the British Navy at them; you'll see."

"The Navy will get them before they land." I certainly hoped so; I didn't like to think about trying to send Nan away; I wasn't sure she'd go—and where could I send her if she would?

"Of course they will," she said. And we let the topic slide. In those days if you had doubts, you kept them to yourself.

We checked several days' worth of papers, and I'd almost decided there would be no more information, when, as I was reading Nan the follow-up to the burnt-toast killing, I saw a tiny brief: "There have been no further developments in the case of the Hyde Park corpse, according to Chief Inspector John Mordren." No, just the absurdity and irrationality of the universe confirmed in a line.

"Well," said Nan, "that's something. A chief inspector. That casts a different light. They'll maybe pursue this after all."

She must have detected something in my silence, for she added, "You'd better tell me about him."

"Who? Damien? I told you, just a boy I saw in the clubs occasionally."

Nanny was not deceived and shook her head. "You asked about the investigating officer."

I tried for airy indifference. "I've seen him around," I said. "I was afraid he was onto the roulette wheel."

"It seems he's onto murder, instead," said Nan. And she gave me a very close look. "You mind yourself. You can't trust policemen, no matter how high up they are."

I went to Soho the next afternoon as soon as Nan and I finished the royal calendar (ho-hum) and the crime news (now a genuine interest).

It was early for Soho. The restaurants were open, but the bars and clubs were either shuttered or losing their looks in the glum daylight. I hit several places before I found Connie nursing a whiskey in a narrow, dusty room made gloomier by a fog bank of smoke and the thick, greenish glass of the windows. In the aqueous light, he looked thin and depressed, his marceled hair lank and greasy; he smelled of patchouli.

"Buy you a drink?"

Immediate brightening; then he saw it was me: he'd been hoping for a quick visit to the park, a romantic afternoon, a splendid night, and a rich, indulgent protector—all the boys were. The belief that someone would come to change their lives was their huge weakness. It kept them waiting and drinking somewhere between hope and despair.

I sat down and ordered a glass of what now passed for wine—with France gone, even the cheapest vintage was precious—and another watery whiskey for Connie, who likes spirits. He could certainly use some.

"Any more on what happened to Damien?" I asked after a suitable exchange of gossip as preliminary.

He shook his head. "Cops don't care. You live in Soho, you're on the game—just less work for them in the long run, isn't it?"

I nodded. Had to agree. "Though it's a bloody shame, that," I said.

Connie sniffled and rubbed his nose, then glared at me, his eyes dark with grief. "Nobody cares," he said. "You—you don't care."

"What do you mean? I didn't know Damien well, but I liked him. I surely hate what happened to him."

"Surely," mimicked Connie. "But how does that help him? You say 'too bad,' everybody says 'too bad,' but you don't do anything about it. See, that's the difference. You really care, you do something, isn't that right?" He put his hand on my arm—stubby fingers; long, pointed nails; a surprisingly strong grip.

He was right, of course. "There's only so much you can do," I admitted.

"Depends, doesn't it? There's only so much *you* can do, right, but now I'm a different case, because I bloody well care." He finished his drink and, preemptory in his grief, demanded another.

"All right." I nodded to the barman. This was another side of Connie: sorrow had turned a page and brought up a whole new picture. "I can understand why you feel bad. You won't get another mate like Damien."

He put his nose in his glass and seemed to calm down. We talked for a few minutes about Damien's virtues, his pretty ways and miserable luck. "And you know," said Connie, touching the waves in his hair and fiddling with a barrette, "he'd been put in the way of a good thing."

"Really?"

"Money in it. He bought me champers."

"Champers is always a good sign," I agreed.

"And more to come. That's what he said."

"This an ongoing thing?" I asked casually.

"No, but steady work. Parties, I think." He made a face and added, "He was a selfish bastard. You'd have thought he'd have said, 'And I have this mate . . . .' Wouldn't you have thought that? Wouldn't you?"

"It's lucky he didn't. Think of it that way, Connie."

"We'd have been all right together. Two of us, we'd have managed. Nobody'd mess with the two of us. You don't think so, but I have ways. Damien, oh, right, Damien wouldn't hurt a fly."

"A Buddhist, was he?" I said, trying to get him to a more cheerful place.

"They don't kill flies?"

"Supposedly all life is sacred."

Connie gave a sour laugh. "Sure it is. Just the same, in the park, nights, it's better to have a mate with you."

I agreed, though I didn't necessarily believe it. "It must be a nuisance with the police 'round asking questions. You get one of the brass, one of the inspectors?"

"You're pulling my leg. Some sergeant. A change from the vice cops, anyway. These coppers are strictly business. With the vice boys, you never know what they'll want—but you can guess. Either way, it's not doing the coppers any good; no one knows anything."

"Still, you must have some idea. You were close to Damien."

He shook his head. "Damien was a hard-luck bloke, that's all there was to it." He tipped up his glass and found the bottom of his whiskey.

"And just when he'd had that piece of good fortune recently. It seems a shame to let opportunity go to waste."

"Maybe it won't." Connie gave me a sly look.

"You know the man?"

"I think I know how to find him, yeah, I think I do. But you won't mind if I keep that to myself, will you?"

I could sense his hostility; there would be no profit in pressing the issue. "Just be careful, Connie. If Damien wasn't killed where he was found, maybe it didn't happen in the park at all."

"Is that what the coppers think?" Anger reappeared in his voice.

I nodded. "According to the paper."

"What do the coppers know? What do they know about Damien or me or any of us? What does anybody care?" He broke into sobs, the tears washing his mascara in two black lines down his cheeks. "You. You buy me a drink, but you don't care. You'd like to know, maybe cut in on the business? Right? I know you—you're after something. I know that much; everyone is. But I can take care of myself."

I excused myself and consoled him as best I could to the tune of two more whiskeys, but Connie closed up like an oyster. In the following days, the press abandoned Damien's tiny, pathetic story, and though I kept an eye out for my cop, his heavy presence, like some psychic barrage balloon, had suddenly shifted to a new locale. Even cruising the park I didn't spot the bulky silhouette, the tweed jacket, and northern vowels. Gone. Damien's case was apparently shelved and forgotten. Perhaps the inspector had been assigned an entirely new and more promising case not requiring visits to Chelsea. Good.

In the inspector's absence, I felt that I had come out from under a shadow, and to celebrate I headed for The Pond one dark, cloudy night after my shift. Forgive the weather report: Without streetlights, we'd all become sensitive to meteorology and conversant with the phases of the moon. Soon we'd be watching the sky like druids and dreading the white nights we now welcomed.

Halfway along, my torch's light began to dwindle, and though I switched it off to save the batteries whenever I could, within a few blocks of The Pond, it petered out for good. I stood swearing for a few minutes, angry at my own carelessness, because the torch had been wavering for a few nights, and frustrated at the thought of picking my way back through the darkness without enjoying the possibilities of the evening. Overhead, the leaden night sky was several tones lighter than the black silhouettes of the buildings. *Returning were*, as Macbeth says, *as tedious as go o'er*. Indeed! I crept at first; then, after negotiating several cross-streets and successfully avoiding a pillar box, I was striding confidently along near the park when suddenly I pitched forward, my useless torch bouncing onto the pavement and my hands scraping the cement. I found myself lying on the ground, half the wind knocked out of me and with my legs sprawled across something at once firm and yielding—and wet. Wet and sticky.

I got to my knees in a spasm of revulsion. I had fallen over someone on the sidewalk, someone who must be gravely hurt, someone bloodied. My lungs contracted with the shock and left me too breathless to shout. I pulled myself up, wiping my hands on my uniform and struggling for air, then I knelt down again. Short hair, a jacket, a man. I whispered to him, between my own gasps and wheezes, "Are you hurt? Are you all right?" I felt for the pulse and touched—in a moment of pure horror—a wound, a wound in his neck. I shook him, rubbed my hands on his jacket, his tunic, something military, some insignia, something pointed, but in my confusion I could make no deduction beyond that this man was dead, surely dead, as dead as Damien, who drank at The Pond and wore violet eye shadow.

I should have made a run for it and literally washed my hands of the matter, but there are dangers in training. While my own common sense said run, my tin hat and ARP badge said report. The nearest phone box was far behind me, immensely far in my current state of advanced breathlessness, but The Pond was a block farther, and thinking of nothing except breathing and reporting, I struggled down the street. Twice I tried the wrong steps before I found the basement entrance to The Pond. A pause at the bottom to stave off panic—there is no panic like suffocation. Draw in air, breathe, breathe, force open the airways, keep breathing.

The door, then the blackout curtain, there: the pay phone just inside the entry. Luckily not in use. Coin, fumble for the coin, hear it drop. Call in. Location a block from The Pond on—gasping—get it out. Address given. "Police. I need the police." Registered; understood. Then name. HQ wanted a name, my name. But here, after so much folly, common sense triumphed. As the pips sounded for more money, I set down the receiver. I saw that I'd left a red smear on the phone and another, the mark of my hand, where I'd held myself upright against the wall. I scrubbed both with my sleeve and staggered from the booth to a questioning look from the hairless, moonfaced barman behind the decorative glass screen.

"On duty," I managed to say, and shoved aside the blackout curtain, as heavy as the suffocating contraction of mucus and muscle in my chest. I stumbled on the basement steps, risking a redder darkness, and crawled the last two or three, almost losing my tin hat. With a frantic gulp of air I reached the street and lunged into the night.

It took me several hours to get home—a nightmare of curbs and lampposts, of unseen lorries and sudden cars, of my emptied, struggling lungs and tortured airways, and everywhere the many varieties of darkness. In the grip of a thousand claustrophobic dreams, I found myself afraid to stop and barely able to walk. I was close to collapse when I heard the sound of water and knew I had reached a little park. The collection of railings for scrap metal has provided a number of benefits, and this green precinct was now open to the public. Low-edging hedges of privet and box scratched at my shins as I made my way along the gravel to a small fountain, where I washed my hands and face, rubbed the front of my stained uniform, and listened to the water bubble until some of my stolen breath came back.

With the faintest new light in the east, I turned west and walked home. Nan was in the kitchen, bedded down as usual on the table. She heard the taps at the sink—and probably my wheezing, too. Nan had sat up countless nights in my childhood after contact with my father's horses and dogs touched off my attacks.

"What time is it?"

"Very late," I gasped. "I need your help, Nan."

She sat right up; as she always says, she sleeps like a cat. "Put on the light."

"Don't be scared. Not my blood."

"Another road accident?"

"Not this time." I told her, of course, wheezing out the details as best I could.

She was of two minds about my speedy exit. "It all depends on whether we can get the blood out."

"I dropped my torch, too," I said, thinking of fingerprints. "I had a serious attack."

"Everyone has a torch these days. You can use mine. Cold water," she added as I started to heat some water. "You need cold water for that. Soak it well and rinse it."

"The uniform will still be wet tomorrow."

Nan shuffled over to the coal stove and put the iron on the hob to heat. "We'll press it dry, dear boy," she said.

It was much later, drinking tea and watching the steam rise as Nan ironed my wet uniform that I remembered the pointed insignia—symmetrical, pointed, possibly wings? Possibly RAF? If so this body would not be ignored, because alive, he had been worth a fortune.

CHAPTER FOUR

They came in the early afternoon. I'd gotten out of bed late after wheezing and gasping and contemplating ruination until midmorning, when I slid into uneasy dreams of enormous doorless rooms with low ceilings where thick, inescapable blankets lay heaped on my chest. I woke at noon with the light moving behind the trees and sparrows chirping. "Nan?"

No answer. I'd been aware of her several times—a small, newly fragile silhouette in the doorway from the studio to the bedroom. Watchful. She can judge an attack as well as any doctor. "Nan?"

Off to the butcher or the greengrocer's or maybe for the paper; she can still read the headline placards at the newsagents. I pulled on my trousers and stuck my feet in my shoes, major effort. My lungs, beyond congested, had turned to suet and weren't fit for much but Christmas pudding. When I bent to pick up my shirt, the world obligingly darkened, producing red corollas around the bureau, the bed, the straight chair. "Nan?"

I stepped into the studio, where my new canvas waited on the easel. A dark limousine with a biomorphic form screaming in the driver's seat surges from a deep orange ground, toward the viewer. The figure was not right yet. Not quite. Something about the foreshortening of the elongated neck, but in my tattered condition I couldn't conceive a fix. There was something odd about the studio, too. A good big wheeze of air to focus the mind: the perfume of damp wool, redolent of nights in the park and just-cleaned uniforms? No, not just. It was the table set for lunch. We always ate in the kitchen, but Nan had covered our "roulette table" with a cloth and set out the lunch things, complete with cutlery and a note stuck under the salt. Her handwriting, once a pride, was still small and well formed but prone to run away at odd angles. *Hope you feel better. Back soon.* I realized that the roulette wheel had disappeared. Then I heard the bell. Had Nan forgotten her key?

Three more rings before I managed the length of the studio and the small hall that adjoined the kitchen. "Forget your key?" I gasped, and opened the door. Chief Inspector Mordren shadowed the doorway like a barrage balloon; at his side stood a spiffy uniform with black hair and mean amber eyes. At a better time I'd have felt a real interest in him, but my lungs shut down, reawakening halos of reds and greens. The Asians think life is a dream; I think our nightmares become reality. Here was mine, police on the doorstep, some dreadful confinement threatened, and Nan out and too blind to read any message they might allow me to leave.

I couldn't speak for wheezing.

"May we come in?" Oh, the inspector was polite, but then he was my personal cop and though he might not have known it, we had things in common. I was still uncertain whether that was an advantage or a danger.

I stepped aside. "May we come in?" was definitely better than "Come with us, sir."

"You live here?" He was looking into the studio. Propped against the wall, a dark canvas showed a writhing biomorphic shape; the orange painting with the limo and its inadequately foreshortened passenger sat on the easel, and a heap of slashed canvas occupied the foreground. Maybe not the best accessory under the circumstances.

"Kitchen," I pointed. "Bedroom at the back."

The uniform was dispatched to check out the studio and the bedroom beyond. The inspector looked into the kitchen. "You're in Air Raid Precautions?"

My uniform, pristine and only slightly damp, was hanging near the stove. "Fool even a butcher's dog," said Nan when she'd finished. The inspector sniffed as though maybe his nose was keener. "It's just been cleaned."

"Nan likes to keep everything fresh." I spoke with a gasp and a rattle and added a little shrug to indicate the mysteriousness of the feminine mind. A terra incognita for the inspector, too, I guessed.

"You're what—twenty-nine?"

"Thirty-one, actually."

"Not in the military?"

"Exempt. Asthma."

"Quite a bad case, I see."

I dropped into one of the kitchen chairs.

The inspector took the other. "With your health, you must always be careful about your living arrangements. If you take my meaning."

I caught a whiff of courts and jail and looked as unconcerned as possible. Thanks to the rigors of life with my esteemed father, I'm inured to bullying.

The inspector turned brusque. "You were on ARP duty last night until eleven twenty p.m. Is that correct?"

"Yes."

"What did you do then?"

"I decided to have a drink at The Pond." I did not give the address, and he did not ask.

"Where you used the telephone?"

"That's right." So they had recorded the number—and my friends at The Pond had spilled the beans. I'd expected better of them. If you can't trust low company, civilization's finished.

"And where you were seen leaving the phone booth," he ostentatiously consulted a tiny notebook to show this was all duly entered as evidence, "'in a fine state.'"

Just so. I could see there was no point in dissembling. They had me "red-handed," as Nan liked to say, literally so in this case. "I was having a severe asthma attack, and I'd just called in the report of a mutilated body. I was entitled to be 'in a fine state.'"

"That's no excuse for not leaving your name. As you should have done as reporting warden."

"As an off-duty warden, I was merely a concerned citizen, who could hardly breathe and was out of change."

"You were obligated to wait for the police. Fortunately the dispatcher thought he recognized your voice. Otherwise, we might have regarded it as a prank call of a particularly despicable nature."

"I'm telling you, I was panicked for air; I nearly collapsed on the way home."

"Where perhaps you had Miss Lightfoot—that is your companion's name, isn't it, Miss Jessica Lightfoot?—wash the blood from your uniform? What conclusion might be drawn from that?"

Let your imagination run riot! But he had Nan's name, which meant danger. I restrained myself and said, "That as an ARP warden responding to road accidents, I frequently need my uniform cleaned."

"How fortunate you have an old retainer to do that for you."

"Nan is—" I started to say, but shut my mouth. What Nan was to me was no business of his.

The inspector sat as motionless as a toad, his hooded eyes half closed. "I believe you also knew the late Damien Hiller. You bought drinks in his memory at The Pond the night after he was murdered."

"I buy drinks for quite a few people when I'm flush."

"But you did know him."

"He was someone I saw around. Look, you were at the other end of the bar. I was trying to cheer up poor Connie."

The inspector's lips pulled back from large and crowded yellow teeth. I'd have given a lot to have been able to paint that peculiar smile. "I have no doubt that your fingerprints will match those on the torch we found beside the body." A dramatic pause. I hadn't realized police work required such theatrical gifts.

"It would be surprising it they weren't. I've already told you that it was my torch—" But here I had to stop a minute to squeeze more oxygen up my protesting airways. I realized that the stress of keeping my lungs topped up was distracting me from the precariousness of my position. If the man had been dead a measurable time before he was found, I was in the clear, no matter what The Ponderous inspector cared to imply. But if not—I postponed consideration of that for the moment. "I literally fell over onto him. Blood everywhere."

"How could you fall over him?" The inspector simultaneously raised and deepened his voice for an effect very different from his soft and hopeful tones when we'd met in the park—or his hoarse viciousness afterward. "You had a torch and he was lying smack in the middle of the sidewalk."

It's unpleasant how the most minor misadventure can lead to catastrophe. Here was another proof of the precariousness, if not the malice, of the universe. "The batteries died a few blocks from The Pond. Check them, you'll see."

"It was a black night," he said. "You'd have been in territory you know well then?" His precision instrument sounded confidential now. "The Pond, the vicinity of the park?"

"Where I believe I've seen you." I stared back to assure him that, although in much physical distress, I was not afraid.

Something flickered behind his small, shadowed eyes, and his hand shot out and grabbed the front of my shirt. He brought his face close to mine and there could be no mistake: This was the dark silhouette from the park. "Be careful, Mr. Bacon. No matter how this ends, your life is so irregular an immorality prosecution is ever a possibility. Remember that."

I said it was the sort of thing that would stick in my mind.

He looked as if he would like to strike me, but he released my shirt and fell back on sarcasm and insinuation. "So you just happened to fall over him."

"I fell over him, dropping my torch, which was useless anyway." Another interruption for energetic wheezing. "In the darkness, it was quite horrible and the shock played up my asthma."

"And then?" He was able to suggest the deepest skepticism in the fewest words.

"I felt around in the dark and realized I'd stumbled on a man lying dead."

"How could you be sure?"

"When I checked the pulse in his neck, I discovered that he had the most terrible wound." I forbore to mention my recollection of Damien or to reveal that he had haunted my dreams.

"Getting the blood on your hands that was noticed at The Pond."

"He might have been alive," I said. "He might have been helped."

"You could be charged, you know," the inspector said.

"On what possible grounds?"

He shrugged heavily and remained silent, provoking me to speak. A trick, that.

"I certainly should have given my name, but if I'd had anything to do with the man's death, why would I have reported it? Besides, I'd only just left my ARP post."

"Unfortunately for you, the victim had not been dead long. The timing would be close. Very close, so you would do well to take this seriously."

"I took last night seriously and I'm barely breathing."

"You might be risking your life daily like the RAF boys."

"Ah," I said. I knew where this was leading. "Damien Hiller wasn't worth a toss, but lose an airman—Was he perhaps a pilot?"

He leaned forward eagerly, quick as a snake: "How would you know that if you hadn't a light?"

"I felt the insignia."

"A difficult explanation to believe," he said with some satisfaction. "But you'll understand the ramifications, the pressure on the investigation for quick results. You'd do, you know. People are as often convicted for what they are as for what they've done. In your case, 'gentleman's companion,' large sums lost at gambling—"

"What about 'public acts of immorality'?" I asked angrily. "Are you putting those on the docket as well?"

His hand shot out again and connected with the side of my face, knocking me off the chair onto the floor. "Things could go hard with you," he said, standing up, and I would have been hit again but for the appearance of Handsome with the amber eyes. Inspector Mordren looked up, unclenched his fists, reassumed—hypocrite toad that he was—his air of calm and control. I glanced in the speckled mirror behind the sink and saw Handsome shake his head. The inspector frowned, waving his hand in dismissal. I got myself off the floor and back onto the chair. Clearly they hadn't found the pot of gold or the rainbow's end or anything that suggested I spent my off hours on homicide. I leaned back in my chair and crossed my arms. I had a tin hat and a badge and a military exemption. Unless they thought to check under the lunch dishes, there was nothing suggestive in the flat. They'd thought they had me, but they didn't. Frightening me hadn't worked and searching the studio hadn't either.

"Well, Inspector, will that be all?"

"Oh, not by a long shot," said the inspector. "I have the suspicion that Miss Lightfoot might be more helpful. She is at this address, is she not?"

Clearly he didn't know Nan! "Miss Lightfoot is a nearly blind woman in her sixties—not exactly a good candidate."

"No, but I might fancy her for disposing of evidence and as an accessory after the fact."

My lungs went into a spasm and I began coughing violently. The inspector watched me with his impassive face and small, hard eyes. I was just getting my breath when we heard the rattle of Nan's key in the door. Why hadn't she stayed away? Why hadn't she gone for a cup of tea and one of those little cakes she likes? Or sat in the park and thrown crumbs to the pigeons?

I didn't hear her cheery call of, "I'm home, dear boy," just her characteristic footsteps with the slight shuffle that keeps her safely in contact with the floor, the ground, the treacherous unseen basis of life—how could I have forgotten the latter for even an instant? And with her, another heavier foot. A second uniform, short and bandy-legged as a jockey, came in with his hand on Nan's arm. She gave me a stricken look and shook her head.

I jumped up. "Nan, what's wrong? What's happened to Nan?" I asked the officer. "Did she fall?"

"Just in a manner of speaking, dear boy." Only a certain thinness in her voice suggested any distress. I hoped they didn't notice; they'd go for any sign of weakness.

"We intercepted Miss Lightfoot this morning at the left-luggage room at Victoria Station," said the inspector.

"He conducted an illegal search, and he shouldn't have been here without a warrant, either," Nan said stoutly. "I can see you've taken advantage of my sick boy, but I know my rights. Herr Hitler hasn't landed yet."

The inspector turned to me. I realized that his ponderousness was partly theatrical, a created gravitas. "Would you be surprised to know we found a roulette wheel in her possession?"

"He would not," said Nan quickly, "for he intended to paint it."

The inspector frowned.

"For a gambling subject," I gasped. I looked rather desperately into the studio at the biomorphic form on the dark ground. "I was going to put the wheel in the background there, a rather abstract wheel, symbolic of chance and fate. Connected to the figure with—" There was the problem, my perennial one of relating figure to background, to the depthless abyss.

The inspector showed his strong teeth, as if he was not much interested in either the meaning or the technique of art. "You'll not get much inspiration from a wheel in left luggage," he said.

"It might have created misunderstandings," said Nanny. "If you visited."

"Oh, so we were expected. You managed to dispose of the chips, I reckon. We were just lucky we'd been following you."

"Might as well live under the Nazis," said Nan, who has a bit of a temper.

"That might be misconstrued," the inspector warned. "But in any case, Jessica Lightfoot, I am arresting you on suspicion of running a gaming house."

My lungs shrank to the size of a tennis ball. "You can't do that. Nan had nothing to do with any of this." I started to gasp and I put my hand on his arm.

"I can have you for interfering with a police officer," he warned.

"But you can't arrest Nan, not for this. She had nothing, nothing at all—"

"I thought that you were supposed to be a homicide detective," Nan interrupted. "You should get on with that instead of following old ladies. We have men left lying dead in the street. What have you been doing about that?"

"Now, that's another matter of considerable interest. Mr. Bacon was seen covered in blood shortly before the body was found."

"My dear boy is often covered in blood. These frightful road accidents. It's all been very badly planned. In the blackout, everyone's as blind as I am, and what's the point? It's not as if you can hide London."

"You admit, then, that you helped him clean his uniform?"

"Don't think I'll be of any assistance if you're arresting me."

"They're not going to arrest you, Nan."

The inspector nodded and Handsome took one of Nan's arms.

"Don't touch her."

He gave me a shove and I started wheezing but blocked the doorway. "You're not taking Nan. Not now."

There was a brief, humiliating scuffle involving a kitchen chair and a great deal of shouting before I found myself in handcuffs with Nan beside me in the back of a police car.

"Did they find anything else?" Nan whispered.

I shook my head.

"Call Arnold," she said.

CHAPTER FIVE

My uncle had a phrase, "down the rabbit hole," used as a synonym for disaster with strong suggestions of the surreal. More on that later. This uncle was a relative of my father's and cut to the same physical mold: a big, robust, red-faced, strong-legged, straight-backed ex-soldier who liked eating, drinking, and smoking—preferably in swank hotels with underage boys. The latter was not known to my father when, after a little contretemps with my mother's lingerie, I was dispatched to the Continent in the care of this bluff, deceptive old roué. The hope was that I'd come back straight and ordinary and fit for good society; didn't happen. Instead, I spent time with Uncle Lastings in a fine old four-poster at a top-flight Berlin hotel, and when, tiring of my reformation, he left the city, he considerately left me penniless and on my own to continue my education.

I've kept the phrase, though, and here was occasion to use it. I'd gone "down the rabbit hole" from my studio, with a promising painting on the easel and (leaving aside my ARP duties and Herr Hitler and the possible onset of mustard gas) all right with the world, to a dank, insalubrious room furnished with a table, two chairs, a green-shaded suspended light, and a solid steel door. No window, *naturellement*. The room, like the rest of the station, was filled with an essence of anxiety, smoke, and sweat that lacked sufficient oxygen for my particular breathing apparatus. After my futile resistance in the flat, I had a throbbing head, courtesy of Handsome, and an inflated lower lip, which I owed to the bandy legged uniform who'd collared Nan.

I didn't know what they'd done with her, a worry eased only by the conviction that I was their real interest. But for what? Footsteps in the corridor, the creak of the door: I was about to find out. In swept the inspector, bringing his storm clouds with him like some Wagnerian deity. I found it hard to think of him, subsumed as he was for me in his role, as a man with a surname, never mind some Christian appellation. He sat down without a word, had a good look at me, and lit a cigarette.

"You're a bit the worse for wear."

"I adore the masterful type," I said, and winked. I couldn't resist. I expected another smack, but the inspector merely frowned and said, "Your life could be made most unpleasant."

Well, well. Could I hope for a nonviolent interview? Had something—or someone—cast a new light on my case?

"I thought," he continued after a moment, "that we might come to an understanding."

"Being birds of a feather?"

"Being rational, sensible men. Remember, I don't have to put up with either you—or the old lady."

"You queered the pitch when you involved Nan."

"I think, rather, that we hit for a six. I can see you don't want your old nanny confined."

"Where is she?" I asked, betraying my anxiety despite all my resolution. "You're not really going to charge her, are you?"

"That all depends on you."

That's what I mean about the rabbit hole: negotiating Nan's freedom with a police inspector whom I had no reason to trust. "I'm not going to confess to murder, if that's what you're hoping. I had nothing to do with the man I found. Nothing. As for our previous encounters—" I left that dangling. I hadn't a clue to what he wanted or whether I had any leverage.

"A confession is not expected at this time. You realize, Mr. Bacon, that we already have plenty for a prosecution. The roulette wheel alone, not to mention obstructing an investigation—yes, not giving your name was serious—and, of course, public immorality. There are people," he said, dropping his voice into a Plutonian register, "who would be happy to testify against you—for some considerations in their own cases. Remember that."

"So much for English justice."

"Like it or not, we need to settle this case quickly—and by any means necessary."

"But what does all this have to do with Nan? Would you release her today?"

"That could be arranged. But be assured she could be arrested on gambling charges at any time."

And doubtless me, too. "If it's not gambling and it's not the murder case, what's all this for, then? You came into my studio, knocked me around, arrested Nan—what was all that for?"

He hitched up his trousers and put his elbows on the table. "You have a number of interesting contacts. People of, shall we say, peculiar sexual tastes."

"Everything about sex is peculiar when you consider it." I do really believe that.

"I dare say we'd all be better off without it, but this isn't a philosophical discussion. We're looking for a sadist of a particular sort."

"Ah. My gentlemen of the peculiar tastes were keen on riding crops. A few whacks on the bum, that sort of thing. I'm not such a fool as to deal with anything else."

"Unlike Damien Hiller."

"A boy of limited brain and delicate health. Desperately poor, too.

But your airman—poor, maybe, but not destitute and probably clever and healthy."

"He's not your immediate concern," the inspector said quickly.

"Are they not connected, then?" Wheels within wheels in this matter.

"Of course they're connected." He seemed irritated by the idea.

"But this man had his throat cut."

"We don't release all our information to the public," the inspector said in a superior tone.

"You expect me to help you find whoever killed Damien?"

"We're looking for a sex killer who operates in or near the park. And we think you can flush out our man."

"Oh, right. Aside from risking the tender parts of my neck, how am I to do that with my nightly ARP rounds?"

"We'll have a word with your post about tonight. A severe asthma attack with emergency assistance required is a plausible excuse. Beyond that, you'll just have to cope. There's a war on, you know."

Didn't I just! "What about Connie? I don't know his last name, but he was Damien's best mate. He told me that he knew how to get in touch with a good 'prospect,' the piece of luck Damien had just before he was killed."

"We're aware of Connie. Colin Williams. He hasn't been seen around the last few days. See if you can find him. Maybe express an interest, a generalized interest in—well, you'll know what to say. Maybe you've got a broken heart, maybe you've got a wandering eye, maybe you're leaving the alderman—oh, yes, we know about him, too. And other things—so watch your step."

"If I were you, I'd dangle Handsome as the bait. You'd catch a far bigger fish with him."

The inspector grunted. "Handsome, as you call him, has other interests."

"Lately some chaps have been discovering new interests." Those were my favorites, but I didn't go into that with the inspector.

"You're exactly what we want, someone sophisticated, cultured. You can fit in places that boys like Damien and Connie and my officers can't."

"We're looking up the social ladder then? Adverts in the *Times*?"

"You might try the Gargoyle Club, too."

"Mostly dancing on tables and late-stage alcoholism there. Boringly safe otherwise."

"I'm wondering about some sort of private offshoot," the inspector said carefully. "Perhaps someone, or some group, that makes contacts at the Gargoyle."

Possible, I thought. Well, off to the old Gargoyle. This might not be so bad after all. "I'll need some pocket money if I'm to drink there."

To my surprise, he stuck his hand in his pocket and hauled out a handful of guineas. "Don't overdo," he said. "Call me every day. And Bacon, don't loiter on this. I might be lenient with the old lady, but I've got more than enough on you any day of the week."

That's how I became, thank you very much, an official police informant, a snitch, a grass, a traitor to the right thinking and free living. At a word from my cop, the steel door opened, a car was summoned, and Nan and I were transported back to the studio Wonderland-style. I was profoundly relieved to be burdened only with the prospect of drinking at the Met's expense, but Nan was not best pleased. I had nasty bruises on the side of my face, plus the swollen lip.

"You've taken leave of your senses," she said. "They had nothing that could be used in court, nothing. Isn't that right?"

The law is a vast mystery to me. "I think they could have kept us locked up for quite some time, Nan. And what would my ARP post do without me at this time of crisis?"

She rolled her eyes. "Nonsense. Arnold has pull. He'd have gotten us out."

"He could have. Whether he would have—"

"Ye of little faith," said Nan. Like the inspector, she felt that my heroic resistance had been unnecessary. "Your devotion is the light of my life, dear boy, but you tipped your hand and put yourself in their pocket."

"Mixed metaphors, Nan."

"They had no evidence."

"They have the wheel."

"I just didn't see them behind me," she admitted. "Though it would have been worse if they'd found it here. They can't link you to it and I doubt the evidence would hold up anyway without a warrant. And the chips were gone. You'll paint out the table. They can't hang us for a case of Champagne and artistic license."

I agreed.

"Well, then. Something didn't fit for you," said my nan, the crime connoisseur, "time of death, manner of death, place of death."

"Very likely, but they'd have gotten us for something just the same. Not to mention the horrors of the law's delay."

"They'd have nabbed you for the very thing they want now," she conceded. "And how you'll go on the town in this state is anyone's guess."

"Most likely they're out of their senses and down the rabbit hole, Nan."

"Without doubt this smells funny."

"It smells like a rat," I said.

On this note of agreement and suspicion, I went to the studio, where I painted the carefully ruled roulette table a dark green enamel that hid the lines with one coat. Nan insisted on a meal, and then I went to work on my battered face. A base of foundation and enough eye shadow to soften the bruises, a good slather of lipstick. I'm partial to lipstick; there's a particular scarlet that I find delectable, a color nearly impossible to reproduce on canvas. And thinking of canvases, I must admit to being tempted by the inspector, who seems to have increased in bulk, inflated by his new and frightening importance in my life. I'm taken with his brow ridge, his thick nose and thin lips, his subtly corrugated skin, the rounded, heavy shape of his face, a shape like my own. I would like to paint him in his interview room screaming, and perhaps I'll get to see that if I'm not successful. Either way, a project best postponed for the moment, when I am to be charming and attractive—"All right, Nan? No smears, no flaws?"—and also subtly damaged and possibly damageable. Handsome helped me out on that.

"Good as can be under the circumstances," said Nan.

My life's motto. "Think of something to tell Arnold," I said and felt guilty before the door had right closed. Arnold's been good to us, and he's genuinely fond of me, but the sooner I came up with something to satisfy the inspector the better, and Arnold's presence would certainly be an impediment.

Given this ruthless and realistic frame of mind, you might expect that I went straight to work, asking questions, trying to locate Connie, comparing notes with other boys who consort with gentlemen. That's what Handsome would have done, and if the inspector had wanted that, I suppose he'd have made different plans. I went out drinking, instead. I stopped at the Europa, where Maribelle—"I'd given you up, cunty!"—scolded me for my absence, and on to a little pub where I met a muscular Gordon Highlander, willing—for one of the Met's guineas—to follow me to the park. Ah, the long English summer twilight, the majestic oaks and elms, and especially their shadows with damp grass and thrashing bodies. I was born for war and disruption, sensuality and disaster; they've been with me all my life: troubles in Ireland, the Great War, and now the prospect of death from the sky and other mortal novelties. I know how to survive, and, besides, we all need distractions while we wait for Herr Hitler.

I got to the Gargoyle late and well liquored, smelling of sex (that excellent aphrodisiac), and looking reckless. Out of the drizzly darkness and into the palace of art and decadence with its mirrored walls and Matisse murals. Yes, by the great man himself. Not my favorite, though his portraits are fetching and his colors priceless. I just don't recognize his world: flowers and pattern and light and *bonheur.* I'm out to paint the rabbit hole full up to the top with violence and absurdity.

"Buy you a drink, darling?"

An angular face like the thin end of a spade, thick eyebrows, an unruly thatch of dyed red hair ill suited to his olive skin and shadowed cheeks. But duty before pleasure. "Music to my ears!"

To the bar, to glasses of prewar wine. He was in the theatre, did lighting and design; once in a great while he "assayed the boards." Nothing impressed me until he began to speak of ancient drama, of the great Aeschylus, and I forgave even his hair. We agreed that *The Oresteia* is a great family drama and a profound political play. And on our favorite scenes, too: the arrival of King Agamemnon, Clytemnestra's account of the murder, the recognition of Orestes. It was, the red-haired man said, his dream to play Clytemnestra but—here he shrugged—the Greeks were not in demand and, in any case, the great days of the theatre ended the minute women stepped on the stage.

"Still," I said, "there must be the occasional production or reading?"

"Yes, yes, but even there"—he leaned forward—"they prefer the feminine look."

Between Aeschylus and decent wine, I was feeling giddy. "Well, the hair's a start," I said.

He frowned, then laughed—a big, braying laugh at odds with his mincing gait and languid gestures. "You'll do, you'll do!" He exclaimed, then he buried his nose in his glass and turned melancholy again before launching into his vision for staging *The Agamemnon*. Fascinating, really. First-rate ideas for the whole trilogy.

"Not to forget the Furies," I said. "Who are with us always."

His ideas about them involved some genuine Kabuki gestures that resembled something between the use of a nine iron and a flyswatter. "The Japanese theatre is so stylized, so eloquent."

"I've always thought the Furies were the key to the whole thing. The mortal characters die and vanish, but the Furies remain."

"Indeed," he said, giving me a shrewd, sharp look. "Indeed, they do." At the same time, I sensed he was not pleased that I had interrupted his explication, that I had ideas of my own. After several more minutes and a provocative, if salacious, idea for the presentation of Athena, he asked if I liked Brighton.

I regard Brighton with horror. The sea, for one thing—deep, wet, and monotonous—and the rows of terraces filled with holidaymakers and landladies. "Like a vision of the afterlife," I said.

"Pity," said my companion. "Money to be made in Brighton." And without another word, he turned to the man on his left, blond and very inebriated, and began once again discussing the decline of the theatre and the thwarting of his life's ambition to portray Clytemnestra. Right.

On several subsequent visits I kept my eyes and ears open and my glass topped up. Though I flirted with a variety of punters and wound up compromised in the gents with a few, I had little to report beyond a substantial bar bill. Oh, there were all manner of deviants—some far outside my tastes—and a good many pleasant chaps who wanted to buy me drinks and fondle my bum, so to speak, but I uncovered no dubious assignations or homicidal depravity.

The whole enterprise seemed pointless. For one thing the Gargoyle, despite its many enchantments, was *haut bohemia* and never the natural habitat of boys like Damien. For another, I felt guilty about Arnold, who'd been leaving me notes and messages that I'd ignored. One night, I turned around right at the door and set off for the gaming clubs. Luck was with me. Half an hour later, I was drifting down a curving stair overlooking the bright rafts of the roulette tables. There in the smoky gloom was Arnold, leaning over the board looking sad and hopeful. I went to stand behind him.

"Any luck tonight?"

He gave a start and turned. I saw a kind, wonderful smile that instantly soured. "I thought you'd found someone new."

"In a manner of speaking. I've been going steady with the inspector."

"You should have told me," he said when we were out at the bar, and I'd given him a brief summary.

"They had the wheel."

"Nan told me that."

"She cleaned out the studio but—well, they more or less threatened all three of us with prosecution."

"Dear boy!" He put his arm around my shoulders.

It seemed I was forgiven. From then on I started taking nights off to meet Arnold again at the gaming clubs, where we lost money and lamented the loss of our roulette wheel. Somehow the inspector got wind of these little excursions, and I was forced back into harness with a visit to The Pond. It had been off my list for some weeks, for, besides the fact that the inspector was convinced the trail led up the social ladder, I had hard feelings about being betrayed by my old drinking companions. But strolling back from Soho one fine Saturday afternoon, I passed the basement steps, heard music, and looked in. The smoke was permanent, the cloud in place though the bar was nearly empty. When I set my gas mask on the counter, the pale and wizened barman poured me a glass and expressed pleasure at my return.

I allowed it had been quite some time. "Under the circumstances, though—"

He nodded. "Still, you might have done it, you know." He spoke with the enthusiasm that Nan reserves for capital punishment. "No, no, you can't tell even with people you drink with of a night. You can't blame the boys for being skittish."

I took this under consideration. No doubt the story of how I had entered the lobby staggering and smeared with blood had undergone many elaborations and enlargements. But now I saw a way to turn this to my advantage. "Have you seen Connie about? I wanted a word and I keep missing him. In case, you know, he'd had any doubts about me, what with Damien being his best mate."

The barman pursed his lips and shook his head. "Not been in for some time. He was off to Brighton, he told me."

"Brighton?"

"Sort of a dirty weekend at the seashore."

"Connie hardly needed to go as far as that. Whatever's in Brighton?"

"Coastal defenses."

"Oh, I suppose. Connie had a taste for uniforms. Still—"

"That's what he said, anyway, and I haven't seen him since." He spoke abruptly, as though my questions had aroused some further doubt, and moved down the bar to top up a drink. Brighton, dreadful place; you can hear the surf rumbling through the shingle. I was almost home before I remembered the red-haired man at the Gargoyle. *Do you like Brighton?* I'd thought it an odd non sequitur at the time. And something else, bring it back from the sea of Chablis where so many ideas founder: *Pity, money to be made in Brighton.* Would I now be expected to venture to the coast, to indulge in some ghastly contact with the beach? I certainly hoped not. Just the same, obtaining the first piece of information was oddly exciting, and as I stepped into the phone box, I wondered if the inspector had felt the same little shiver when he saw the blood smears on the wall and found my discarded torch.

CHAPTER SIX

"Brighton," said the inspector. A pause down the line as if he were thinking it over. Put into words, my discovery was an airy nothing, and waiting in the phone box, I expected heavy weather for wasting police time. Not so. "You don't think it's a club?" He asked finally.

"I don't know. Could be either, could be both."

"Find out before you go. No, no," he responded to my protests of work, my ARP duties, Nan's difficulties, "we'll contact the Brighton police about Colin Williams, but you move in the right circles. If this theatrical chap is in Brighton, you'll have to go. Give me his description again."

I repeated the distinguishing characteristics of the redhead from the Gargoyle. Initially, the inspector had not been impressed, and I'd had the fleeting hope that other evidence had turned up to make me superfluous. But when I explained that the redhead's favorite role, Clytemnestra, wielded a big knife, the inspector brightened up considerably. "Sniff around the artsy circles," he said in conclusion. "Someone's got to know. This is good work."

Given my history, I get suspicious whenever some one tells me I've been a good boy, and this matter struck me as more dubious than most. I couldn't imagine Damien in Greek theatrics, and I didn't see "Clytemnestra" trading her big Mycenaen knife for some sort of bludgeon. Still, the inspector was pleased, and his approval would keep Nan and me out of jail.

The next morning, I knocked off work early to visit my old friend Roy, a barrel-chested Australian gifted with moderate talent and inordinate charm. When I returned to London after my continental adventures, he not only taught me the rudiments of oil painting but also introduced me to everyone I would need to know. For lines into what the inspector called "artsy circles," Roy was the man. He worked near Victoria in a big studio cluttered with his bold, bright canvases and magpie collections and still furnished with a few elegant, if wretchedly uncomfortable, pieces I'd done back in my designer days. Lately he'd been working on portraits of both Arnold and me, providing a perfect excuse for an unannounced visit. When I arrived, Arnold's portrait was leaning against the wall to dry, and, first thing, Roy wanted my opinion.

We stood studying the canvas, Roy in a characteristic pose with one hand on his massive head. He impresses one as a cheerful person, quite without shadows; his work strikes a darker note, both in the bold, intense colors and in what I can only call a subtle foreboding. He had Arnold to the life, but he'd caught a certain skepticism, at once worldly and wistful. This was not an expression I saw very often, but was one I now realized must be there. Though a hopeful gambler, Arnold was old enough to know the odds—in wagers and in life. It gave me a little turn to see that captured.

"It's very good," I said.

"You sound doubtful."

"What does Burns say? 'If we could see ourselves as others see us . . .' I think that goes double for one's lovers. It's good. Really."

He smiled; he'd thought so too, but studio light is often deceiving. The work one loves turns out to be junk, while some little unconsidered piece, on further review, has possibilities. "And now for the pendant. You've come for a sitting?"

"Is that all right? I was at a standstill this morning and I thought—"

He made me welcome as always. We exchanged art-world gossip and tales of the blackout and the ARP while he got out the canvas, adjusted his palette, and checked my pose. I kept an eye on his rather high-toned colors, the cadmium reds and yellows, both raw and burnt sienna balanced with cold raw umber, and an array of vivid greens and blues, the intense colors of his continent. "You need to be looking straight ahead—that's right. Excellent, excellent," he said with a smile of anticipation; against all the odds, he finds my face inspiring.

"Face like a pudding," I said, but Roy's painted me before, and my studio, frequently. The most unlikely people and images can prove useful. I understand that.

While he worked, Roy chatted to keep me diverted. Now and again he frowned or puffed out his cheeks or stopped to stare intently at my features. I have a completely different approach. In between sittings I like to work on portraits from photographs, and I like to finish up with just the canvas and the image in my mind. When we took a little break I mentioned the red-haired Aeschylus fanatic I'd met in the Gargoyle. "I never got his name. Would you know him? A theater designer, I think."

"Very thin, hawkish face?"

"That's right."

"A bit of an old queen?"

"Did you know these are Kabuki gestures?" I flounced around the room and made him laugh.

"That's him. His name's Aubrey Teck. I'm surprised he didn't ask you to join the group."

"I fell from favor by disliking Brighton."

"It is very prudent to dislike Brighton, though I personally like the piers and the Royal Pavilion. Haven't you ever seen that? Oh, Francis, really! It's Moorish fantasy— an opium dream without a pipe. All shut up now, I should think, for the duration."

"But what was this group?"

"I think it was the Brighton Group, the Brighton Club, Brighton Drama, something along those lines. He's always on the lookout for likely boys for fun and games. I couldn't imagine how he was getting them with that dreadful hair, but drama, I suppose, that is something different."

"He longs to play Clytemnestra; he sees a great career ruined by the advent of actresses."

"I shouldn't doubt," Roy said, and laughed.

"A harmless enough ambition, I reckon."

"Daft, simply daft, darling. High drama in sheets with gestures." He waved his arms in the air. Despite, or perhaps because of, a proper education, Roy is not as taken with the Greeks as I am.

"Where did this group meet, do you know?" I tried for casual; with all his contacts and acquaintances, Roy functions like an artistic town crier, but his antenna detected my more than passing interest.

"Don't tell me you have theatrical leanings. Oh, dear, squelch that; it's painter's ruin."

"Not me. A friend of a friend is desperately keen on Greek tragedy," I said, though I doubted the inspector would agree with any part of that description. "When he heard about Teck, he wanted me to check him out."

"Well, your friend will have to head to Brighton. Of course, my dear. Why else would it be called the Brighton Club or whatever it is? It's definitely Brighton Something." Roy had what I think of as an antipodean laugh, coming from somewhere in his capacious belly and utterly infectious. After a certain amount of banter, I had not an address but tips on a few likely pubs and a general idea of Aubrey Teck's Brighton habitat.

I might have gone straight to the inspector with this gen. Like that? More military slang: "general intelligence"; Liam keeps us up to date on all the latest. Except this intelligence was hardly general, and I was leery of handing over even Aubrey Teck to the inspector on such slender grounds. No. What I did was invent another asthma episode for the ARP post and got Arnold to run down to Brighton with me.

I told him I was convinced there was nothing, nothing at all, in the business and no reason to put Teck in the way of the police. At the same time, a journey on the crowded trains to Brighton and an effort to locate the Brighton Something-or-Other of Wild Boys and Greek Drama would be a serious effort, maybe enough for the inspector to move on to other prey. I was joking when I said that, but many a true word is spoken in jest. There was something predatory about my personal cop, who more and more struck me as a man of two sides, neither of which was in good contact with the other. My importance lay in the fact that I was in touch with both the man who picked up boys in the park and the copper who arrested them. It behooved me to be careful.

"Come see this, dear boy."

I stretched my arms and got up from the big carved bed with its creamy, luxurious sheets and fat down pillows—shades of Berlin and Uncle Lastings—and went to where Arnold was standing at the tall hotel window. The sky was dark and rather stormy to the east, fading red and gold to the west: spectacular Turner effects, now too impossibly beautiful for a serious painter. One of the little tragedies of modern life is that scenic beauty has become problematic, and the Brighton sky was nothing if not scenic. Down below was another matter. The hotel overlooked the pebbled seafront now strewn with rolls of barbed wire and studded with cubes of concrete as protection against landing tanks. Vaulting over both, the piers strode far into the sea on their long spider legs, their bulbous pleasure domes gradually darkening as the blackout commenced. We could hear the sound of pebbles rolling and rattling in the surf.

Arnold draped one arm across my naked shoulders and recited, "*The sea is calm to-night. The tide is full. The moon lies fair upon the straits . . .* " He is fond of poetry. "You don't know 'Dover Beach'?"

I didn't know "Dover Beach."

"Apt, maybe too apt: *Listen! You hear the grating roar of pebbles which the waves draw back, and fling.... With tremulous cadence slow, and bring the eternal note of sadness in.* Sophocles is in it too. Though not Aeschylus, our present interest."

He recited the rest, though the only lines I can remember are: "*Ah, love let us be true to one another*"—perhaps Arnold's hope for me—and the ending: "*And we are here as on a darkling plain. Swept with confused alarms of struggle and flight, where ignorant armies clash by night.*"

As Arnold said, too apt.

"Of course, he wasn't thinking of invasion, but of the decline of Christianity, of faith in general."

I leaned my head on his shoulder and listened to his ideas about the poet. Arnold regrets my neglected education and is keen that I should be knowledgeable, that I should miss nothing, that I should be complete intellectually. If my father had spent half—even a quarter—as much time on me as Arnold has, I'd be a better man by far, perhaps one capable of fidelity and other impossible virtues.

But this was not, as I know the inspector would agree, a time for virtue! A drink or two with Arnold, a little paint, a little powder, a little Kiwi polish in my hair—I like to go dark for night—white shirt, black trousers, black leather jacket.

"Don't tangle with the gangs," warned Arnold, who feared the notorious Brighton toughs who prowl beneath the piers at night and fight with razors and bicycle chains, pastimes I regard as both exciting and ridiculous.

A few kisses for Arnold, who was off to see a friend in Hove, before we went down to the lobby, bright with lights and gilt, and out to the darkening streets. This is a time I like. The sky is still light enough to silhouette the buildings and distinguish people on the pavements, but details are lost in shadow, and I can feel the shyness and regrets of my life begin to dissolve in darkness and in alcohol. To the pubs, then! To drink with nerved-up airmen and sailors and violent, thin-faced men of no certain occupation, possibilities on every side! Alas, tonight I have a special quarry. One pub, two: a fine mix of bored men, painted women, and ambidextrous boys, but no Clytemnestra and no Connie, my second target, either. Dancing with a Polish airman, blind drunk, who did the complicated figures of some ancient Slavic dance. Discussing Monet with a bearded Scotsman who nursed a whiskey as if it were the water of life and had heated opinions on the Impressionists in general, Monet in particular. "He should never have left off figure painting. Never."

An interesting idea. One I'm willing to entertain.

And now, my mind in an interesting place after four pubs and assorted libations (a good Greek word for a night seeking Greeks), streets dark with touches of deepest purple and brown, a drizzle rain beginning, the sea whispering in my ear like all the bad ideas of my life, I enter—where am I entering?—the Hound? The Greyhound? Some dog anyway, a bad omen; dogs are the bane of my life, seizer of my lungs, hounds of hell. Through the curtain, lights, smoke, laughter, smell of perfume, painted faces, falsetto voices, promising, promising. A drink. Chablis, real if sadly watered; still, a good omen, and the gods suddenly turned favorable, for as I am chatting to a muscular chap in black leather pants finished with a bicycle-chain belt, I hear someone say, "Disaster, total disaster. The production's a total and complete loss. And darling, I was so ready! *At once, at once let his way be strewn with purple, that Justice lead him toward his unexpected home.*"

It could only be Clytemnestra. I patted my companion's arm and slid away through the mix of khaki and pastel frocks and leather. I saw the vivid red hair above the hawk face. Aubrey Teck was heavily made up and wearing a dark-feathered tiara with an ordinary lounge suit. "*The rest a mind, not overcome by sleep, will arrange rightly, with God's help as destined,*" he declaimed.

That is the end of Clytemnestra's welcome speech to her husband, and, stepping behind him, I replied, "*I tell you to honor me as a man, not god. Footcloths are very well; embroidered stuffs are stuff for gossip. And not to think unwisely is the greatest gift of God. Call happy only him who has ended his life in sweet prosperity.*"

"Darling!" shrieked Teck. "Come with me!"

I don't think he remembered me from the Gargoyle; his eyes were very black and dilated. The inspector, no doubt, would have labeled him "in a fine state," but now that Teck had a likely Agamemnon, one, moreover, who knew at least the famous lines, he was flying high. He had what he called his little pied-à-terre, a flat in a big terrace not far from the pub; "a quiet neighborhood," he assured me. He mentioned the tranquility of the area twice, although I was uncertain that was a recommendation. I found Aubrey Teck deeply unattractive, but the dark streets, his urgent hand on my arm, the silhouette of his feathered headdress produced a certain frisson, accentuated when we arrived at a massive, neglected-looking terrace. The heavy door creaked open on a dark foyer with a shiny black-tile floor and a hint of bad plumbing. An unseen kitchen was at the back, bedroom probably to the left. On the right was a large, dimly lit lounge painted a deep maroon with what my ARP-trained eye noted were first-rate blackout curtains and shutters. It was sparely furnished with a fireplace equipped with candles, and, below the single bare ceiling bulb, a claw-footed bathtub with dubious stains. An unlit standing lamp in the shape of a brazier cast a properly archaic shadow on a long runner of purple carpeting—the footcloths of Agamemnon, no doubt—and, hiding what looked to be the sole chair, big swaths of red and buff drapery. Voilà: the never-before-glimpsed interior of the palace of the House of Atreus. Clearly this would be an unconventional production.

Aubrey indicated an antique breastplate and a length of unbleached linen. "Clytemnestra requires a little more," he said. "I'll sneaky-weaky off to change. There's some wine."

Sure enough there was a bottle of sherry, heavy with sediment, on the mantel and a pair of strange cups like martini glasses that had been half melted and flattened. I took a good swig before checking the tub, which had, I noticed, a drain pipe and a water supply, though a big ceramic pitcher stood beside it on the floor as backup. Nice enough for a bath before the fire, though hardly reassuring for Agamemnon, given that Clytemnestra kills him in his tub. Another swig of sherry—

it really was dreadful stuff and possibly adulterated. Detecting an unfamiliar aftertaste, I spat into the fireplace.

But, as Nan likes to say, in for a penny, in for a pound. I took off my leather jacket, discarded my clothes. The heap of linen resolved itself into a kilt and an oblong cape with a big round fastening pin. Kilt first, short enough to expose tender parts to the breeze. Breastplate next, light and mercifully nonmetallic, as there was a distinct chill in the room where fire, and even the past summer's warmth, were only distant memories. Papier-mâché with handy elastic straps, the breastplate was clearly some theatrical prop. The cape next. Over one shoulder, fasten with the big archaic pin. On the back wall, light wavered in a full-length mirror, and there I was, despite the pudding face and a tad too much lipstick: King Agamemnon, loyal brother, great warrior, bad husband, worse father.

"Come to the door."

I turned. Aubrey was standing in the doorway wearing a full-length gown of some purple stuff trimmed with gold. He was adorned with several large necklaces and the dark-feathered headdress that to me was more Queen of the Night than Mycenaean. I walked to the hall. He held up his hand, pointing to a spot at the edge of the purple runner. When I was correctly positioned, he swirled his gown and with one imperious gesture, became Queen Clytemnestra.

"But it is the conqueror's part to yield upon occasion."

"You think such victory is worth fighting for?" Was that the line?

"Give way. Consent to let me have the mastery."

"As I step on these sea-purples may no god shoot me from afar with the envy of his eye." I couldn't remember the rest, but I saw it did not matter. Clytemnestra was deep in the moment, her eyes fathomless, her motions ritualistic, perhaps drugged. I wasn't feeling too steady myself. Down the carpet toward the fatal bath while my homicidal queen declaimed to the imagined audience in the foyer.

" . . . if only its master walk at home, a grown man, ripe.
O Zeus, the Ripener, ripen these my prayers;
your part it is to make the ripe fruit fall."

The whisper of sandals on the rug. We were obviously dispensing with Cassandra and the chorus of nervous and ineffectual elders. Clytemnestra stalked in and turned on the tap to fill the water pitcher. With many gestures, some doubtless inspired by the Kabuki theatre, she motioned for me to undress for the Returning Hero's Ritual Bath, or RHRB in our modern, military-inflected terminology. I hoped Aubrey had remembered to put some coins in the water heater.

Off with the cape. Off, with the queen's assistance, the breastplate. I suspect the real Clytemnestra got on with things a bit faster than Aubrey, who seemed keen to explore my anatomy. No matter, the farcical, the erotic, and the sinister were now so intermingled that my head was spinning. Into the tub, cold on the bottom, in both senses. Water poured, lukewarm—might have been worse—then, suddenly, something rough and stringy over my head and arms, a net. Instinctively, I threw up one arm and tried to stand but I was struck in the middle of the back. I gave a cry, more surprised than hurt, Agamemnon's lines forgotten. "Let me up!" I yelled as I tried to get my feet under me. Clytemnestra shrieked in response and a second blow knocked me back so that I slipped on the wet porcelain and struck my head on a tap. I had time to hear Clytemnestra breathing hard and to feel something wet and sharp against my chest before a woozy blackness obliterated the sense that I'd made a dreadful mistake.

Breathing and gasping, stray shrieks of pleasure or pain dying into a silence broken by the rustle of some long, feminine garment. I was clearly not dead. There was a lump on the back of my head, and I explored it unhampered by the net. Not trapped, either. I opened my eyes and almost passed out when I saw the dark river spilling from my shoulders to my groin. A bad scare provoking bad, bad memories. Living on one's own in early youth exposes one to violent lusts and the drift of one's own blood. I was on the verge, balanced on the sharp edge of nightmare—the worst, the waking kind—when a quick check of my throat proved the skin intact. Belly, and all parts below, likewise. I was definitely not dead. A deep breath brought in the scents of Clytemnestra's heavy perfume, bad sherry, a fair whiff of mildew and drains, but not the abattoir stench of blood, the authentic odor of the House of Atreus. A play then, all just a play, or say, rather, a fetish of the most elaborate type, and the darkness that had nearly pushed me into my own bad dreams was some dramatic trick, such as a man of the theatre like Teck would surely know. Another deep breath and I turned on the taps. Bad idea. Cold water poured down my back, so icy that I almost hopped straight out. But cleansing, definitely, as a wash of red stuff ran off my back and shoulders and swirled down the drain with a burp and a gurgle.

Clytemnestra was nowhere to be seen. She had disappeared, along with Agamemnon's costume. A pity, that, as there was no towel. I shook myself dry as best I could, untangled my bundled-up clothes, and dressed. I was debating whether to rouse the Lady of the House of Atreus or vandalize the lounge or give vent in some other way to all the disquiets of the evening when I discovered that several new pound notes had been left in my jacket along with a note: *"Best production ever!!!!"* I detest the excessive use of exclamation marks, don't you? But the pounds looked good, and it was much in Aubrey's favor that he paid both promptly and generously. Roy's assessment came back to me: *Daft, simply daft, darling.* About right.

"I don't think he's the one," I told Arnold when I returned to our room very late, very damp, rather sticky. He was sitting up in bed, reading the newest Ambler thriller, and as I hung up my leather jacket, I heard him gasp. "You're all-over blood!"

"Damn, my shirt will be ruined."

Thoroughly alarmed, Arnold got out of bed. "All strictly theatrical," I said, though when I took off my shirt, the better hotel light revealed a multitude of scratches from Clytemnestra's long nails. "Quite safe, if thoroughly weird."

I washed myself in the sink and left my stained shirt to soak while Arnold recounted the much-less-dramatic nightlife of Hove.

"No sign of Connie, I suppose."

"Not a peep. And you know, he may be using another name."

"What makes you think that?"

"It may be the done thing," he said, pointing to one of the many cards pinned up along the front: MISS CHERIE, FOR THE TIME OF YOUR LIFE. "How many English girls are christened 'Cherie,' do you think?"

How many indeed!

CHAPTER SEVEN

Seagulls woke me a few hours later—another of the reasons one should avoid the shore and other natural habitats—but spared me the continuation of a bizarre and unpleasant dream. I was tempted to be incommunicative, to pick a quarrel with Arnold, to behave badly. He ignored me and rang for breakfast. When it came, wheeled in on a large tray replete with silverware and covered dishes, sparkling china and fine linen, everything steaming hot and smelling wonderful, I burrowed out from under the covers and decided to be cheerful. I love breakfast in bed at all times, providing the bed is luxurious and the company good, and now real jam, real coffee, real butter—once unconsidered trifles—were an epicurean feast.

There were kidneys, too, in wine sauce, and haddocks swimming in butter, which I love, and two perfect eggs—wherever were they getting them?—and proper little hotel racks of nicely done toast. Arnold has taught me how to eat properly and to appreciate good food, and I have done him proud as a pupil. Of course, with the wartime shortages, one didn't need anything elaborate to be amazed, just ordinary unadulterated food like the lovely poached egg I shoveled onto a piece of beautiful real wheat bread.

I found it impossible to stay irritable after such a start to the morning. We went back to bed for a while, and when we got up, Arnold bought me a new shirt. Then, since we had several hours before our train, he wanted to visit the piers, where he'd come as a boy and brought his own children. He had happy memories of the arcades and ballrooms, and breakfast inspired me to make the best of it. As we drifted along arm in arm, I asked likely lads if they knew a boy by the name of Connie. "He wears garnet lipstick and long nails. Blond hair, a flyweight. Seen him?" I made it clear that I owed Connie money and was looking to pay my debt.

A young sailor just off convoy duty seemed a likely prospect. We bought beer and meat pies and sat on a bench all together for a while. He said he'd gone deaf in one ear from the naval guns. He was nineteen and looked five years younger, no bigger than a child despite his rough, swollen hands and thick Navy sweater. I much admired his bright pluckiness and his claim that it was easier for a smallish sailor—that was his description of himself, *smallish*—to get around a ship. He told us about one's life expectancy in the cold north Atlantic—thirty minutes tops—and the new dangers since the German invasion of Norway, but he'd never heard of Connie.

We had no better luck in the seedy little pubs along the front, nor with a group of RAF mechanics stooging about one of the dance floors.

"Most likely he never was here at all," Arnold said. "He wasn't the sort of boy to leave his home ground, was he?"

Not likely, I had to admit, but then Damien's death had unsettled Connie, who had maybe latched on to his friend's piece of good luck. What circles might that entail?

At two p.m., we caught the London train, crammed with khaki, found seats before Horley, and were only delayed twice with air-raid alarms, once outside of Preston Park and again near Three Bridges. We reached Victoria two hours late, not at all bad for wartime travel. Arnold hailed a cab for home, and I rode the Underground, figuring to call the inspector from the phone box near my stop, emphasize my diligence, and get excused from all further efforts. I had just left the tube station and was within yards of the phone box, when Moaning Minnie started. No matter how often you hear it, you feel a jolt when that infernal screeching starts. I broke into a run for home. Though I was sure this would be just another false alarm or minor raid, I didn't like Nan to be alone, and I wanted her to know that I was back safely. With the siren still howling like the lost and damned, I opened our door and called, "All right, Nan?"

"Is it planes, dear boy? I thought I heard engines."

"I can't hear a thing except the siren."

"Look outside."

At the window I saw something metallic moving behind the trees. Out onto the step. Overhead were schools of silver fish. Row upon row of Heinkels, Junkers, and Dorniers with their fighter escorts. Don't be surprised at my aviation expertise—wardens are trained in spotting enemy aircraft. Moaning Minnie was lost in the rumble of their engines, a sound beyond sound that shivered the pavement and vibrated every cell in my body. Already smoke was rising in the east, and people were running in the streets amid speeding cars. This was it, but I didn't believe it. All the waiting, the barrage balloons, the false alarms, the minor raids, the jokes about the Jerries. We'd thought, I suppose, that this particular inconvenient, but tolerable, life would go on indefinitely. More astonished than frightened, I couldn't take in the attack right away; then a shout, "Report to the post! The show's on this time." Liam, of course. Excited as a kid at Christmas. This was the big one after all.

Back inside, I grabbed my uniform jacket and my tin hat. "I've got to report. You'll need to get to the basement, Nan. They're bombing the East End."

"Not likely to bomb Chelsea," she said, but she picked up her mask.

"Where's the torch?"

"You'll need to take it."

I realized we'd never replaced the one I lost. "I'll get you downstairs, and I'll come back for you. If the lights go, don't try the stairs on your own."

"Light, dark makes no difference to me," she said, but she let me take her arm as I counted off the steps. "Down three, turn left. Down . . . five, six, seven, eight. You'll be facing the door to the lumber room. One, two, three steps, handle on the right. Could you manage it yourself?"

She shoved the door; on her second try it opened to the dim basement with piles of trunks, old bicycles, and rubbish. A thin gray light seeped in from one small, high window that had never been fitted for the blackout. Not that it mattered now; they'd found us anyway.

"Stay away from the window. And use your mask at the first hint of gas. You'll be all right, Nan?"

"You go ahead, dear boy. Be careful."

I kissed her cheek, closed the door behind me, and raced up the steps to keep away bad thoughts about leaving her in the darkness. I was wheezing by the time I hit the street and saw the young secretary who lived upstairs, running full tilt in her high heels.

"It's a raid," she shouted. "It's real this time. It's real; we're going to die." She was white around the nose and mouth and near panic.

"Go to the basement," I said in my best warden voice. "Nan's there. Look after her for me."

Oh, the power of a tin hat and a badge: The girl took a big breath and got hold of herself.

"Nan's downstairs?" Nan was a general favorite.

"Best place. You'll be safe from a blast there." I didn't know about gas. If gas came, we might all be finished, masks or not. I actually stood there for a minute, calculating the time of exposure, the margin of safety, but I still wasn't frightened. Except for anxiety about Nan, I didn't feel anything. Not then.

The young secretary shouted to a plump, flush-faced girl in a spotted dress—funny how clearly I saw the details, the white ruffle at her neck, the red buttons—who had run herself out of breath and was holding her side. No panic now in the magic of a plan, even one as defective as this. "Hurry up, Esther. We're to go to the basement."

I hurried off though my sector, checking the rows of houses. Children running for home or gawking at the planes or clinging, weeping, to frantic mothers trying to maneuver infants, prams, purses, shopping bags, and favorite toys to safety. Men in shirtsleeves, disturbed at their Saturday chores or football scores, shouted questions. I shouted back, pointing, directing, dodging cars and bicycles. *Shut off the gas. Electric, too. Leave house doors open for blast!* A few were in hysterics, weeping with panic; most calm, needing only direction, a reminder of the nearest shelter; some carried masks like sinister piglets. *Use your Anderson shelter. Go down to the basement, the tube station, the crypt. Go to ground like a fox.*

I hoped to hell that was right. Gas is heavy and falls like a blanket onto your chest, slides into your eyes, and coats your lungs. But bombs get you on the surface and hit the upper stories first: no good choices. There was the butcher in his striped apron—I sent him to our basement, dubious company for Nan!—and further on, discovered the newsstand boy huddled under the roof of the kiosk, still at his post. "Take cover! Now! Tube station's closest." Even then, in the midst of my warden's duties, I was having trouble with the reality that we might all be minutes away from annihilation by some toxic cloud.

By the time I reached the wardens post, having doubled back to be sure that there was no one left unprotected, thick columns of dust, smoke, and fire billowed to the east; they were hitting the dockyards. The sky was filled horizon to horizon with flights of bombers making a queer, uneven drone like a million drunken bees. Where were our guns? Our fighters? Nothing. Nothing but the floating barrage balloons as our guardians. I could smell the odd mix of sweet and sharp from the burning wharves and warehouses as the goods of London went up in smoke.

Inside our HQ, a cramped room in the basement of the Geological Survey Museum, everyone was milling around, desperate to act but uncertain what would help and trying to look busy as commands and suggestions flew right and left.

"Blackout's not going to get done," one of our wardens was shouting.

"No matter now, they'll navigate by the fires," said Liam.

"More important to get people into shelters."

"No good if there's gas. We'll need stretchers, burial details." This was an old major, a veteran of the Somme, another for whom the Great War was an eternal presence.

"Any reports yet of gas?" That was our head warden. Another vet, a sergeant, but younger, less marked; short, ordinary in every way, but a natural leader. He and his wife, Joan, ran the greengrocer's on the corner and shared the work at the post. Calm and smiling, she made up gallons of tea and catered the baskets of sandwiches. He had the gift of organization; as soon as he took control, we fell into place—a talent, that. "Everyone's sector checked?" We reported as he read off our names. "You all have your lists?" We did. If we took a hit, we'd use our lists to canvass the survivors and discover the missing.

"We get a bomb in our area, we're out. Otherwise, soon as the all-clear sounds, we do our assessment. Save your energy in the meantime. Francis, see if you can keep the telephone working. Any report of gas, tell me immediately. Someone want to take the roof as spotter? Two—we'll need two, one to report to me if there's a hit, then to Francis, who'll pass on the information to the central HQ."

Right. The switchboard, my useful technical skill. Suddenly the reality of the situation hit home. My hands were trembling, my mouth dry. The battle, so long at high altitude or in another country, had come home to us, and we could all be gassed in an instant. The stench in the air was already contracting my lungs, but no time to think and best not to. Plug in, put on the headset, pencil handy, crackle of the line, start to write.

In the chaos of the first day of the Blitz, I forgot to tell the inspector about Brighton.

Chelsea didn't get hit that day or the next; instead, the Jerries pounded the dockyards and the poor East End nightly for the better part of a week. But though the fiery angel had passed over us, it was only a temporary reprieve. Soon we were all too familiar with the sounds and rhythms of a raid: the screaming sirens, the rush to get our neighborhoods properly sheltered, the thunder overhead. And then the explosions, the bombs that whistled, that fragmented, that doused already-raging fires with oil. Sea mines the size of pillar boxes descended in the night, silent and enormous under their huge parachutes. We learned to listen for the thump of their landing and the serpent hiss of the fuse before the blinding white ball, ringed with lavender, and the blast wave could sweep you off your feet and whirl you like cyclone and leave you in so many parts we had to fetch a basket. That was if the mine went off. If it didn't, major relief was followed by gut-wrenching suspense, with some luckless warden keeping the neighbors back and guarding the thing until the bomb crew defused it.

These fiery armaments surprised us; we'd been all trained and equipped for gas with gumboots and masks and eye shields and gas-proof coveralls. But what we got was fire, infernal and spectacular, the night sky lit up like a Turner seen on opium. One of the worst bombs was the smallest: the thermite incendiary. It looked like a stick and rattled down by the dozens. You'd hear the distinctive plop-plopping as they went end-over-end down the slates before bursting into violent bluish-white flames. Incendiaries snuck into roofs through chinks and gaps and flamed unseen in the blackout until the rafters caught. Soon a house or flat or terrace that looked cold and solid had swallowed the fatal flames, and another street was caught in a howling fire wind.

Those were the raids. In a raid, your adrenaline is up, and you see and do things without thinking much, because they have to be done. You stand next to your own imminent annihilation while your fellow warden lights up a fag and complains that there's no pub nearby. Or you lift off a beam and see a crushed child without a minute to mourn or to find the right words for the frantic parents. Everything's lost in the rush of fire and explosion, in droning planes and shrieking sirens, in the splash and tramp of stretcher parties wading through the dark water left by fire hoses.

Because the distinctive Blitz smell of smoke, high explosives, ancient dust, pulverized wood, and domestic gas seized up my lungs, I mostly worked the phone, checked the shelters, and found housing for bombed-out families, another good way to get acquainted with the price of a raid. But on shorthanded nights I was out, and some nights when the Jerries got started before we had everyone tucked up, yours truly had a ringside and spectacular view. We were busy at our ARP post, and I suppose the inspector was similarly occupied. When we finally discussed my theatrical efforts in Brighton, he seemed uninterested. Mass casualties have a way of putting even gruesome murders in perspective. If my luck had only held a bit longer, I'd never have needed to see my copper again.

Of course, my luck didn't hold: "Call happy only him who has ended his life in sweet prosperity," as Aeschylus so aptly puts it. We had a night of light raids. The ack-ack guns were in operation by that time, and periodically our night fighters—the Blenheims and Defiants—were held off and the antiaircraft gunners switched on their massive searchlights and had a go at any plane caught in the beams. I don't know that they hit much of anything, but it was cheering to hear the rattle and boom of our artillery. You can see that I was developing a properly martial frame of mind. Anyway, a light night. I got off early and stopped to visit Arnold, who was a fire watcher nearby.

Action over the docks again, just enough to light up the sky. The terrible Blitz could be beautiful, and there were moments, sitting up in the church steeple where Arnold had his post, when we might have been watching fireworks in some fabulous romance. Of course, in this romance, sudden death was an excellent possibility, but we'd adjusted to that, and to being hungover with exhaustion, not alcohol, and to sleeping for half an hour at a time and waking up in an instant. Arnold looked tired. He had twenty years on me and the long nights told on him. "Take a nap," I said. "I'll watch for a while."

"Dear boy." He leaned his head on my shoulder and was gone in an instant, leaving me to survey the cratered city. Skies silent now, smoke on the breeze from the dockyards, a dirty fog coming off the Thames. A few hot red spots, the work of incendiaries, but a quiet night, considering. Before dawn, the all-clear sounded and we descended the nearly vertical steps from the spire. Down below, the usual scene—mud, pools of water, broken glass by the truck-load, steaming ruins, exploded gardens. The usual detours for ruptured mains, cratered roads, electrical cables. The usual ambulances, police cars, fire engines. The usual stunned residents gaping at whatever was left; the usual workers beginning the daily trek through our ever-altered landscape.

Arnold had headed home, and I was within a half dozen blocks of the flat when I approached a terrace that had taken a direct hit. It appeared that the wounded had already been taken to hospital, for a warden and several Heavy Rescue Squad workers were standing around looking exhausted, cigarettes drooping from their blackened fingers. The top story of one house had folded up like a concertina onto the lower floors. Everything was smashed but still cold and smokeless, so there was a suspicion that an unexploded bomb was concealed in the rubble. Hence the conference.

When they saw my tin hat in the gloom, they waved me over. A sharp yapping bark greeted me: how often dogs signal bad luck. This was a terrier like the rat killers that haunted my father's stable. It was running back and forth before a mound of rubble topped by a thick and heavy timber.

"Someone still in there?" I asked.

"Might be. That's Jeremy's dog." This from a large, muscular chap, his face totally blackened, a dirty bandage on his right arm. He was the Heavy Rescue Squad leader, one of the construction specialists called in to shift rubble and to either make ruins safe or supervise their demolition.

What could I do but ask if they needed a hand?

Another consultation. Six of us, they decided, might be able to lift the timber. I went through the gate, over a toilet tank and part of a bureau, avoided a framed picture, glass perfectly intact, of Queen Victoria in the Jubilee Year, and a thorny and vigorous gooseberry bush. The squad leader, whose name was Bill, lined us up, cautioning us on the treacherous footing—a mix of shattered wood and crumbled brick.

"On three, lads. One . . . two . . . three . . . "

Muscles straining against the immovable timber. Too heavy, I thought, my lungs already protesting. Then scrapes and rattles as our boots shifted on the rubble and a shout of encouragement from Bill. Timber up. "Bring it to me, step at a time. Swing the front, Robbie. Wait, wait. Now. Watch the damn dog. Let her down." A soft thump from the timber. The dog dived toward the cavity newly opened in the mess of brick and timber before raising an eerie howl. Strange how effortlessly expressive animals are, while we hairless beasts must struggle over canvas and paints and the English language.

The local warden switched on his torch and I followed suit, holding our lights so that the demolition men could do their work. Wall fragments edged with shattered teeth of brick. Another sizeable timber requiring my participation—how we conspire in our own ruin. Another desperate howl from the dog. And then, out of the gray plaster dust, a muscular arm, bloodless and white. No matter how often you see rescue attempts, the moment of recovery always hits you. Sometimes a surge of hope, sometimes, as now, the sick anticipation of horror.

We all got into the act, hauling bricks, sweeping away the dust and plaster, lifting bits of lath. The face, always the face first. No sign of life. Hands reached out to clear the neck. I leaned forward to search for the pulse and stopped.

"What is it? What's the matter, mate?"

"We'll need the police," I said. "He'd have been dead before the first bomb."

A light directly on the wound, a single terrific slash across the throat. *Déjà vu* and memories of the dead airman and the inspector's visits. I could hear my own breathing. And there was another bad thing about this one, now livid in our torches: his light hair, his pudding face and short mouth, his dark brows. It gave me a turn how much he looked like me.

"That's Jeremy, right enough." This from Bill. "Some tart's been his downfall."

"Or some tart's husband," another said.

"Poor Jeremy liked to sail close to the wind. We'll get him uncovered, lads. The police will want to see him."

The Heavy Rescue boys went to work. My fellow warden departed to summon the authorities, and I stood stunned and wheezing beside the dog, who had lain down with her head on her paws to whimper. That's where I was, off my own particular patch and just waiting for my colleague to return, when a reporter arrived, complete with camera. Lots of luck to him—most casualty photos were censored; we all knew that. But, in the perverse way of the universe, this case, being a personal as opposed to an impersonal violent death, was the exception. Some hours later it appeared in the first afternoon edition: MURDER VICTIM FOUND IN BOMBED-OUT HOUSE, complete with photo. Not a morale-damaging close-up of the corpse but a snap of yours truly, complete with tin hat, standing with the faithful dog beside the tarp-covered body.

CHAPTER EIGHT

"It can't be a coincidence," Nan said, peering at the news photo through her big magnifying glass.

"The picture is a coincidence. Wrong place, wrong time," I said, attempting to avoid her implication.

"The picture is bad luck. His resemblance to you—you're sure, dear boy, it was not just the strain of the moment?"

I shook my head, and Nan nodded. She knows my visual perceptions are acute and my visual memory virtually flawless. "And within, what, five, six blocks of us?"

"No more."

"Do think carefully; could you have made an enemy?"

I shook my head. That thought had crossed my mind as I walked home from the bomb site. It's true I can rub people the wrong way and that I'm not afraid of a fracas. I know some rude boys and rough trade, too, but I'm not one to leave hard feelings behind. Not my style. "The demolition workers said Jeremy was an awful one for the ladies."

"Humph," said Nan. "You never know what that kind will get up to."

"It might have been as the locals thought," I suggested, "a romance gone bad, a mad woman or angry husband."

"Might be," said Nan without sounding convinced, "but I'm thinking we'll see that inspector on our doorstep before morning."

A fascination with detectives, fictional and otherwise, led Nan to exaggerate the efficiency of the Metropolitan Police, but she was dead right about the inspector. He arrived late the next afternoon to ask how I'd shown up at the bomb site just before the body was discovered. "That's getting to be a bad habit with you," he said.

With his little notebook—"so Bromley Terrance is not in your assigned sector?"—and his ponderous manner, not to mention the hypocrisy of his personal life, he irritated me beyond measure. Determined to tell him as little as possible, I omitted my visit to Arnold's fire-watching post, allowing the inspector to think I'd left the ARP close to dawn. In retrospect, this was foolish, but although there was no crime in visiting Arnold, "your alderman" to the inspector, I didn't trust my personal copper not to involve him. "A quiet night," I concluded. "I decided to stretch my legs on the way home. I walked a few extra blocks."

He gave me a look. Perhaps he wasn't a walker, perhaps, aside from frenzied moments in the park, he wasn't enamored of the damp night breeze, the grotesque shadows and spectacular lights of the Blitz.

"Did you know him?"

"Jeremy, whatever his name was?"

"Jeremy Gowen." He opened his little notebook. "'The second warden had a very strong reaction to the sight of the body, especially the face.' Why was that?"

"It was just the light, I am sure."

"You've seen bodies before."

"More than I've wanted. But it was the light, a trick of the light. It seemed to me that Mr. Gowen resembled me strongly. It was a shock, on top of the discovery that he'd been murdered."

"Interesting that murder was your immediate assumption."

"His throat had been cut."

"Flying glass creates terrible wounds."

"No, no, I've seen what glass does. This was a single blow; I'm sure of it, positive."

"We will see," said the inspector, "Meanwhile, no more trips to Brighton—or anywhere else. You'll be reporting to your ARP post tonight?"

I nodded.

"Inform me before you travel anywhere outside of London—or even if you should leave your current address."

Right you are, as Nan likes to say. I should have packed my bags then and there, but, led astray by duty and patriotism, I told Nan not to worry and reported to the ARP post as usual. I was barely in the door before Liam gave me the good news that the coppers had been snooping around. "Wanted to know what time we all left last night. It's fortunate Peter's got us organized to sign in and out. I showed him the book." Here Liam nudged me. "I told him you like to go poaching on other people's turf."

I've heard better laughs on the Brighton beach donkeys. But he'd given me fair warning. Early that evening I was having a cup of tea between air raids when Joan stuck her head in at the canteen door and said I was wanted.

"I'm on duty. Who is it?"

"An inspector something and two patrolmen. They're waiting for you at the top of the stairs."

"Thanks. I'll be right there."

Two patrolmen. One was essential to preserve the dignity of the inspector, who could not appear publicly without an aide. Two was another matter, suggesting an imminent trip to the station house, if not arrest. I didn't hesitate. I scooped up my tin hat, my gas mask, and torch—it wouldn't do to be missing bits of the kit—and checked the hall. Joan was headed up the two short flights that led to the main foyer of the museum. I ducked under the stairwell to the custodian's domain and the storerooms, where I followed the yellow circle of my torch the length of the building, past the piping, equipment closets, and mysterious, long-sealed doorways. Here were racks of rock specimens exhaling the dust of the ages; big, outmoded Victorian cabinets, still crammed with minerals; and workrooms with tables and special hammers and chisels for dividing specimens. They would think to come this way, momentarily. Friendly, helpful Joan would say, "Well, there's only the one door," or something like that. I'd surprise them. I took a narrow staircase that gave access to the exhibition hall, eased the door, and turned off my torch.

With the blackout in place, the only illumination came from the entryway, below the wide formal stairs. In the darkness, specimen cases loomed, the size of mastodons, while lumps of minerals like eroded heads stood sentry on display columns. My gumboots squeaked on the hard, slick floor. I stopped twice to listen to the echoes of voices below, to check the faint lights near the entrance. When I heard a clatter, I started to run. They were coming up; I'd go back down the narrow rear stair. Some of the junior staff had offices on the lower level, and I touched the doorknobs as I went along: locked, locked, locked. There had to be someone careless. Had to be. I'd been along here before, exploring during the boring early days before the Jerries got under way with mass murder. A sound somewhere; I switched off my torch just in time, because there was a glimmer of light at the far side of the massive building: the second patrolman, no doubt. I slid along the corridor, door to door; everything was locked up properly. Who did they think would steal their Jurassic or Precambrian specimens, their sediments and igneous and conglomerate rocks? But human life is a constant battle against delusion, and who knew that better than yours truly, who was beginning to regret his oh-so-natural impulse for flight? To have been detained to assist the police would have been seriously inconvenient, but to be arrested for attempting to elude them would be worse, would be, for my inspector, pretty much a signed confession.

I was casting about for some plausible excuse—the sound of a rat was lame, a promise to check the museum blackout only slightly better—when a doorknob rattled under my hand. I almost dropped the torch in surprise, but one push and I was inside. I flipped the latch and switched on my light. A figure leaped out at me: hat, tweed coat . . . no, no, breathe again, clothes on a rack. This was a proper office, teapot on the hot plate, blackout in place on, yes, there it was, high in the wall, a small horizontal window.

Onto the desk, dusty boots on his papers, sorry mate, couldn't reach otherwise. Still couldn't. I jumped down, pulled the chair aside, shoved the desk to the wall. Up again, stretched to my utmost, I fumbled under the blackout fabric for the latch but found the sash swollen shut, showing the occupant's shocking indifference to fresh air and my personal safety. I clawed at the window, tearing my fingers. I was shaking them when I heard footsteps in the corridor and, with a decisive wrench, swung the window up. I pushed my hat and my torch out onto the wide sill and clambered after. I kicked the desk back as I dived though the narrow opening. Hat and torch flew out ahead of me, landing with a bump and a rattle in the darkness below, while I wound up balanced with my head and chest in the night, my hips, legs, and feet sticking up into the office. I couldn't see how far I had to fall, but I wiggled farther and farther out before, losing my pivot point and my balance, I dropped into space. The window banged down behind me.

My hands hit gravel and the rest of my anatomy somersaulted afterward, connecting with something hard on the way down but coming to rest no more than three or four feet below the window. And then, for the first time in many hours, luck: the air-raid siren set up a howl. I sprinted away. A few streets over, I clamped my tin hat on my head and, in the smoke and darkness, started directing folk to the shelters.

In this way, I hid in plain sight most of the night, which, with few clouds and the moon coming to full, was a bad one. Under cover of the raid, I moved through the city, my dusty warden's uniform acting as my credential. I was *on an errand, reporting to HQ*; I'd been *sent to the wrong post; streets were closed* behind me—the Blitz provided plenty of excuses. I reached Soho shortly before dawn. The wet streets were spangled with glass and mucky with earth from bomb craters. The all-clear was sounding when I pounded at the door of the Europa.

A window opened above. Maribelle bellowed, "We're closed, cunty. Fuck off." The voice of an angel!

"It's Francis," I called. "Let me in. I'm in an awful pickle."

"Ha," she said. "When aren't you?" From the depths of the room, I heard Delia, her Jamaican lover, say, "What that little bum boy want at this hour?" The window slammed shut, but after a few bad moments, there was a rattle behind the door and Maribelle appeared with her noble face and hawk nose, straight and imperious even in a threadbare bathrobe like some exiled empress.

"I need a place to hide," I said.

Maribelle gave me a skeptical and appraising glance. Other pickles had left me in a less flourishing state. "And you're in bloody uniform. We've got a uniform, Delia," she shouted upstairs.

"Don't bring her up unless it's a Wren."

"I'd have thought you'd rather have a FANY," I called.

A big laugh from upstairs, but I knew it would take more than that to pacify Delia, a powerful Jamaican who sometimes worked the bar and who was known for her violent and uncertain temper.

Maribelle gestured toward the stair. Above, we bypassed the empty club, so much smaller and shabbier than when it was full of revelers and three deep at the bar with my friends, rivals, and lovers, to reach a bedroom done in flaming pink satin and red-flocked walls like an elderly bordello. Delia, lanky and graceful with long dark limbs under a short nightdress, was sprawled in bed, looking as fierce and exotic as a panther and not much friendlier.

Maribelle nodded toward a round padded ottoman covered in wild gold brocade. I sat down and took off my tin hat. "I'm on the run from the police."

"Oh, mon, police is bad," said Delia. "Why you think we want them here?"

"How bad?" asked Maribelle.

"Do you remember Damien Hiller, the boy who was murdered?"

"Of course. They don't think . . . ?"

"Not him, no, but that's when the inspector got his eye on me."

"Oh, ho," said Maribelle.

"Oh, ho, indeed. And now there've been two more bodies, and, Maribelle, here's the thing. I found one on the street when I was going off duty and the other turned up two nights ago after I'd stopped to help another warden."

"That's awkward, cunty, but it doesn't sound more than awkward."

I explained my difficulties the dreadful night at The Pond.

"What you drinking for in that hole?" Delia asked. "You drink in a place like The Pond when you could be among friends?"

"Momentary lapse in judgment," I admitted. "And tonight. After talking to me this afternoon, the inspector shows up with two coppers."

Maribelle and Delia agreed two cops indicated serious intent.

"So," said Maribelle, "how is it you're not tucked up safely at the station?"

This was my cue. Maribelle's found me amusing from the first day I set foot in the club. I don't know if I've mentioned that I drink there gratis for the pleasure of my company and the custom of my friends, who are many and thirsty. Maribelle likes a laugh, but she is also a businesswoman par excellence. I leaned forward on the ottoman and described our ARP center.

"Not a real uniform in sight," Delia grumped.

"But full of rocks."

"Sounds promising," said Maribelle. "For those of your persuasion."

She had joined Delia on their big and very pink bed. They sat together, arms around each other's shoulders, while I described my race through the storerooms and my frantic search for an unlocked office. I had them both laughing by the time I was stuck half in and half out of the window.

"Then on to my warden's duties. I kept moving toward Soho, my promised land and sanctuary."

I hoped Maribelle would take the hint, but instead she said, "Bloody night. We had to close after the second air-raid warning. Members aren't what they used to be."

"You can say that," said Delia and laughed uproariously.

"I need a place to hole up. I'll sleep on the floor. I'll sleep on the bar."

"You'll sleep in the street cause you'll bring the coppers, mon," said Delia, and even Maribelle, more inclined to mercy, was dubious.

"Best cut a deal with your inspector," she advised.

"I don't trust him. We have a history." Of course, I described our encounter in the park instead of how I'd embarked on a career as a police snitch. I would have been done for with both ladies if they'd known about that.

Maribelle's face clouded.

"Just until I can get a message to Nan tomorrow," I pleaded.

"You crazy, mon. They'll look for you here first. Everyone knows you drink at the Europa. And you crazy, too, girl, if you let him stay."

"What's his name? Your inspector," Maribelle asked.

"Mordren. John."

"Oh, shit," said Delia. Maribelle looked grave and shook her head.

"What? What is it?"

"He has a bad reputation in certain quarters."

"He likes to beat up boys," Delia added with a certain relish.

"This is not news to me," I said. "He banged my head against a tree."

"Not likely to hurt you that way," said Delia. "He beats little white boys black, I heard. Maybe he thought you were with some razor gang. Thought you might come back and cut his throat."

It struck me there might be some truth in that idea.

"There was talk right here at the bar," Maribelle said carefully, "after Damien was killed and the boys found out who was investigating. That's all I'll say."

"Who? Who was talking, Maribelle? I'd better know. I'm going to have to find out."

"Hire a fucking detective," Delia said. "Everything that happens in the Europa is confidential."

But Maribelle appeared to be taking the idea under advisement. Her list of club members is a well-guarded secret, but visitors are fair game, and after a moment, she said, "Came as a guest and hasn't been back lately. George was his name. I think he works as a mechanic, but

John, your friend the photographer, will know. He was all over him. I blush to remember."

Delia laughed at this. There is no recorded instance of Maribelle blushing for anything, ever, but, all right, I'd start with John; I should have thought of that myself. He went everywhere, drank with everyone, shot anyone interesting who came within camera range. "Thanks," I said. "And can I stay for now?"

"Tonight only."

Delia set up a loud and coarsely obscene protest, but Maribelle overruled her in the end. "Francis is an artist. He's going to immortalize me. When we're all dust and the Europa has passed on, there I'll be forever. Right?"

I bowed. I would, indeed, do her portrait, a challenge and a pleasure, if I could keep out of jail.

She threw me a pillow and told me to be up before nine when the charwoman arrived. "You'll have to move on then. Best find somewhere no one knows you."

I felt that I could rely on Nan for that.

CHAPTER NINE

A rattle, the squeal of old hinges, the scrape of swollen wood. I opened my eyes on a sour, dusty morning-after-the-Blitz light. Sat up and knocked my head against the shelf of the bar. Saw a very pink pillow and a row of bottles, heard footsteps approaching: the day jumped into focus. I was lying behind the bar at the Europa, where I had slept on one of Maribelle's pink satin pillows. That uneven step was the charwoman, whom I had promised to avoid. I peered over the top of the bar. A stout, gray-haired woman was stumping toward the WC for her pail and mop. I stuffed the pillow onto the shelf and collected my hat and mask. As soon as I heard the door to the WC close, I jumped up, stinking of dust and beer, and hustled out the door and down the stair in my stocking feet to the street. I pulled on my boots and set off into the morning.

Horns, sirens, detours; dust, smoke, and mist. Workers of all sorts were already picking their way over craters and trenches, trying to avoid gas lines, some broken, and cables, some live. Heavy Rescue Squads were at work on nearly every block, and on one corner firemen sprayed water onto a still-smoldering building—three walls, no windows, roof in the cellar.

I got tea and a cheap roll at a canteen. "Bad night," I remarked.

"I've seen worse," said the tea lady, her face pasty with fatigue, her hair in a kerchief, her sweater stretched and stained: everyone's wardrobe was beginning to look tired.

Back on the street, I was nervous for a bit, seeing coppers and arrest in every pedestrian, but I soon realized I had little to fear in the post-raid chaos. The previous night had left my face black with soot, and I believe that I could have passed the inspector and his handsome sergeant without their taking the slightest notice. With this conviction, I stepped out boldly with a reasonable impression of innocence.

Besides, the eyes of the London public were focused on the newly treacherous ground, the heaved paving stones, the sharp obstacles; we were all busy updating our personal maps in a district where landmarks were routinely altered or erased. There should be a pub on the corner—wasn't that the one with the fine fish and chips? Where was its old-fashioned hanging sign? Gone with the blast, along with the pretty window boxes and whole upper story. And what's this? Usually a convenient alley, a quick detour by the antiquarian and used bookstores, now a massive, steaming, Blitz-reeking heap of masonry.

I took the better part of an hour to reach John's studio, normally a fifteen-minute walk, but my knock still came too early for him. I pounded the door for a good five minutes before he rolled out, whey-faced with black circles under his eyes and a greenish tinge to his unshaven jowls.

"Francis?" He rubbed his hand over his eyes as if I might be the ghost of last night's gin.

"Yes, it's Francis. May I come in, John?"

He looked up at the sky. "I dare say it is still morning, Francis."

"It's around ten. May I come in?"

"At this hour? Afternoon. See me then. Not too early afternoon either."

He made to close the door, but I wedged it open with my foot. "I need your help."

He looked at me blankly. John does not function well in the early hours. Nor the late hours either, though there is a period in between when he makes brilliant photographs.

"I'm being pursued," I said, knowing he loves gossip and scandal.

"Oh, to be young and beautiful. Let him catch you, darling. That's my advice." He again attempted to close the door, puzzled by what was keeping it open.

"Not that kind of pursuit." I glanced over my shoulder for emphasis. "And it won't be good for you if I'm seen here." With this, I gave him a shove and slipped inside. "You're a friend in need," I said.

John looked skeptical. "This is really too bad of you, Francis. Now you're inside and I'll have to put you out."

"I'll be gone in a minute if you'll just listen to me."

But comprehension was too much to expect so soon. "I need a little refreshment," he said. "A little wake-me-up. You're sure it's ten? I haven't been up at ten for years."

"As close as I can determine."

Before I could say more he wandered into the windowless kitchenette and darkroom that serves most of his needs, physical and artistic. He reappeared, bottle in hand, looking slightly rosier. Ignoring my appeals, he went straight to his big portrait camera and swung around to face me.

"Not today, John. Absolutely no photos today."

He put is eye to the lens. "You're extremely filthy and in uniform, too." He looked up in an accusatory way. "Why aren't you at your post?"

"I had to leave suddenly. That's what I'm trying to explain."

"Absent without leave! Naughty boy."

"Very. But John, no photos. And try to remember: I've not been here today."

"I frequently doubt that people *have* been here. My loves have a certain airy, indeterminate quality." His narrow face drooped and threatened melancholy.

"This time I really haven't been," I said. "I need to find someone ever so quick."

"Your busy life! Pursued and pursuing." He took another drink. I hoped that this unseasonably early tippling would not render him completely useless.

"You met an attractive young fellow at the Europa not too long ago."

"I meet so many," he said glumly, "but few are what I'd call attractive."

"This one was. Name of George. I think he works as a mechanic. I need to find him, soonest."

"This is bad of you, Francis, to try to turn your appeal on him. If he's so attractive, you might leave him for me."

"I just need to talk to him. Please concentrate for a moment."

I found a glass and poured him a proper drink. The disadvantage of liking alcohol is that so many of one's friends are drunks. Two glasses later, John had finally achieved his normal equilibrium, and I once again broached my need to find George.

John shook his head. "Don't remember him. Don't. The great passion of my life, and it's gone." He clapped his hand on his forehead and struck a pose. You never quite know when John is serious and when he is just enjoying an attitude. I felt like taking him by his skinny neck and giving him a good shake, but patience, patience.

"Might you have taken a photograph of him?"

A sly smile.

"Have you some recent proofs? The Europa? A handsome boy who's been around? Name of George?"

John said we could but try. I noticed his hands shook as he sorted the various folders, meticulously kept despite the squalor of the studio. "How long ago?"

"Four weeks. Five at the outside. Pre-Blitz."

"You should have said pre-Blitz. All life is divided into pre-Blitz and post-Blitz. *Vita est omnis divisa . . .* et cetera." He opened a folder of night images: the high contrast of electric lights in darkness, laughing faces against windows covered by blackout curtains, smoke from a cigarette hanging like a veil; two graceful boys dancing; another, solo, with blond hair and a surly expression, sizing up the crowd. There was also a small photo, barely larger than a snapshot, of Connie with longer, fairer hair than I remembered and his trademark two-inch nails, which I filched while John was refilling his glass. The photo might prove useful and I don't believe in resisting impulse. The snap was in my pocket before he turned around.

"These are terrific," I said. John has a good eye and the gift of instant perception. He freezes the precise moment when the subject reveals himself. What would that look like in paint? And could I achieve it in oils? One of the big questions of my life.

"George was his name?"

"Yes, George."

He shook his head. I was beginning to think Maribelle had sent me on a wild goose chase, when, half a dozen folders on, he stopped at a shot of drinkers at the bar. I could see he recognized someone. He turned over one more photograph and said, "Oh, that George. Oh, yes! A dainty dish, metaphorically speaking. Physically well put together and all parts in working order." He tapped a photograph of a husky fellow with thick dark hair, straight brows, and narrow eyes; he was smoking a cigarette and staring insolently at the camera. The background was apparently the Europa, and John had somehow caught his subject's reflection in the bar mirror undistorted by the flash.

"Any last name, any address?"

"Frahm. George Frahm. My good Fleet Street training: ID every photograph. He works in a garage in Stepney. Now, let me think." John closed his eyes before he triumphantly picked up one of his grease pencils and scribbled an address. "Repairs motors, he says. Mostly stolen, I should think."

"This is invaluable, John."

He leaned back against the table and gave me a close look. "You're filthy enough to be conspicuous."

I washed up in his kitchenette. When I emerged, drying my face and hands on one of his thin, gray towels, he asked, "So who's behind you? Cops or robbers?"

"Some of both."

"Darling, I am filled with admiration." He pushed himself upright, and retrieved a shabby jacket and a rather dirty fedora from the coat rack by the door. "Nothing you'd ever wear, right?"

He'd read my mind. "And, therefore, ideal. Thanks, John. But I was never here, right? Please remember that."

"You cut someone's throat?" he asked.

"No, but someone may be out to cut mine."

I ventured toward the East End wearing John's hat and jacket, my trousers pulled down over my gumboots and my ARP gear stowed in a sack. Inconspicuous, in a word; within a few blocks I felt quite invisible. I was strongly tempted to take the tube home and reassure Nan myself. However, despite my general philosophy of life, some impulses are to be resisted. I made my way over the piles of earth and gaping sidewalks and around warning lines to the tube and the train to Stepney: another world, worse in every way. Smoke and dust hanging in the air clawed at my lungs, and every step disturbed soft flakes of ash that rose like phantoms. We'd been hit in the West End, but nothing like this, where block after block had been reduced to rubble or blackened by the fire winds sweeping off the blazing docks. Tenements had been opened like sardine cans to illustrate the caprice of the universe: one flat collapsed, blackened, any living thing crushed; the one next door, with the wallpaper unblemished on the remaining walls and the table still set for a late supper. Here a dolly with no more than a smudge on its painted nose; there a little cart, squashed to splinters with the blood of its owner on the handle. A dead horse, probably a peddler's, lay amid rags and blood and bits of flesh. On every block, men and women were clawing their way through the rubble seeking anything they might salvage, while small children sat shocked and disconsolate on what had been the stoops of their homes. Curious boys with pale, underfed faces and streetwise eyes explored the enormous bomb craters or ringed the sinister lines and warnings of the UXB, waiting for some excitement.

The streets I'd known had been replaced by a maze of rubble barriers and improvised alleys, yet here and there were pushcarts loaded with shoddy clothes or old boots or scrap metal or salvage, and even a couple milk wagons and a vegetable seller. I was pretty well lost before I thought I recognized a pub behind the usual sandbags and the taped and boarded windows. I tapped on the door and asked for Wee Jimmy.

"And who wants to know?" asked the publican. He was big, though not as big as Wee Jimmy, but from his ginger beard and thinning hair I pegged him as a near relative.

"It's Francis. Tell him Francis with the wheel."

A burst of laughter. "I didn't know you. Sure if you're not in disguise. Come in, come in. He's shifting kegs in the basement." He turned and shouted, "Someone to see you, Jimmy!"

Footsteps on the stair. Wee Jimmy was perhaps six-foot-four or -five and proportionally huge, a Goliath with a missing eye and a number of convictions. We had employed him as lookout on our casino evenings. I understood that his criminal activities were various, but his nature was gentle, and he was known to Nan and not, as far as I knew, to the inspector. He greeted me warmly. After we sat down with a couple of beers, I told him I needed an errand run—usual rates. When I mentioned it was a message to Nan, he shook his head.

"That's by way of a favor," he said. "You'll do me one in turn. Actually, you've already done me one. Painter, that's what I call myself now. I put on that white kit and I'm bloody well invisible." He laughed.

I explained that Nan needed to find me a place to lay low. This interested him.

"You wouldn't consider—" He gestured around him, meaning the pub, meaning this particular quarter of the East End.

"I might bring you trouble. I need somewhere no one knows me."

"Not a crazy boyfriend, then?"

"More like a crazy police inspector."

"Ah," he said. "You have become entangled with the law."

Le mot juste! "Exactly. And I need to be free to get disentangled."

"Easier said than done."

"I have hopes, but time is of the essence, Jimmy; I can't leave Nan alone for too long. Would you know someone called George Frahm? I'm told he works at a garage around here."

Wee Jimmy's face changed. "You don't want anything to do with George," he said. "Not a man of your parts and education."

I gave him a brief and well-edited account of my troubles. "He apparently knew Damien. I've heard he had interesting ideas on what happened. He might be able to tell me something useful."

"He more like did the job himself," said Jimmy, shaking his head. "Violent bugger. The garage is just a front. His boss is a fence, and George is there to protect the operation."

"He apparently moonlights on the game, though."

Wee Jimmy shrugged his massive shoulders, thought for a moment, then said, "I'd better go with you. No, no, business this, but a good rate for you."

We settled on a few bob and started off, Jimmy swearing at every alteration, every ruined tenement. His own family had been bombed out weeks ago, and he'd lost a sister. "Direct hit. She was under the table right enough; table held, not a mark on her, but she took a heart attack. They'll owe us for this," he said, gesturing toward the steaming wreckage that extended in every direction. Jimmy was something of an expert here. Twice we were stopped by Light Rescue crews eager to make use of his great strength to shift washtubs and timbers, and once by a Heavy squad not quite heavy enough to prop up a wall. Criminal and rescuer, Jimmy seemed to be an informal member of a number of outfits—and who knew what else the war might reveal about him, or, for that matter, about any of us?

The shattered landscape deteriorated as we approached the docks with their pall of smoke and dirt. "We don't know what's left from one day to the next," Jimmy said in a matter-of-fact tone. But though some of the ruins were steaming and a particularly bad section with many hoses and pumps further confused the route, we at last approached an unfriendly little block building with a high metal fence and windowless garage doors.

"Open for business," he assured me. "Of the sort of business they do." Down an alley no more than a footpath wide, Wee Jimmy reached up to tap on a whitewashed window. A moment later, we were inside a cluttered office separated from the work bays by a door with a shade pulled down over the glass. A wizened little man with the eyes of a dyspeptic ferret was sitting behind the desk. It took considerable effort from Wee Jimmy—and what I gathered was a large reservoir of goodwill and past obligation—to secure me an interview with George, who was eventually summoned from the closely guarded interior of the garage. Wee Jimmy and the boss retired, and I was left with the sullen but undeniably attractive and charismatic George.

Fortunately, a glance did it; I knew his type—one of my favorites, though I could expect a few bruises. He pretended disinterest, but I knew better and exerted my charm. Twenty minutes later we were drinking in a filthy pub with beer the color of urine and much the same taste. Shortly thereafter came an interlude in an alley filthier yet. Very unwise, very exciting. Had he carried a knife, he'd have gone to the top of my list, but no, a man for his fists. We sat on a sheared-off stair and shared a cigarette afterward. I mentioned my inspector as a man of similar tastes.

George was offended. He was by way of being a gentleman, while the inspector . . .

"You know him then?"

"Know of him. Sure. I know of him."

I pressed him for more, told him the copper was an exceptional experience.

"You were just lucky," said George. "Sure, he'd be safe enough for someone like me. Don't know about you." Another drag of the cigarette. "Killed a boy, he did."

"You're pulling my leg."

He grabbed me by the throat; sudden swings toward bodily violence were George's stock in trade. "I never joke with strangers."

"Right. The inspector killed someone." He let me go. Sarcasm apparently wasn't in his repertoire either.

"How do I know? That's what you want to know, isn't it?"

A man of real perception.

"Name of Damien. You knew him?"

"We had a drink together once. I noticed he got down sometimes."

George spat at the wall of the alley. "Good for a bit of fun but no fiber to him."

"Consumption will do that," I said. Mistake. Growling and threatening. George clearly liked a little groveling. I complied, then asked, "So what happened?"

"Hit him too hard, that's what."

"Damien was found in Hyde Park," I pointed out.

"Think I don't know about the park? Eh? In the fucking West End that the Jerries are ignoring? But he wasn't killed there. He was killed here. There's this pub with private rooms upstairs where he was a familiar face. Him and the inspector, too. Enough said?"

"Witnesses?"

"You don't believe me?"

Danger ground. "I believe you," I said quickly. "I just wonder, hypothetically now, how it could be proved. I mean, if they were seen together, drinking together even, that will come out eventually."

"Nothing comes out of here," George said. "And now, pub's gone; witnesses too, probably. You and I could be gone tomorrow. Right?"

There was only one thing to do about that, but I did remember to ask him about Connie.

"Never heard of him," he said, and put his hand down my trousers.

"Don't wrinkle my photo." I took it out and made sure he looked at it, but there was no recognition, and none afterward, either, when he took a second, cooler look: Connie wasn't in this particular loop. Or not yet. Maybe the now-conveniently-blasted pub and its brutal clientele had been Damien's secret opportunity. Poor boy. And poor Connie, too, if he'd connected with them as he'd hoped.

Later on, when, minus John's hat and with his old jacket in truly abominable condition, I set out to meet Wee Jimmy, I could declare partial success. I didn't entirely believe George's story, but it was clear why the inspector had kept his eye on me from early on. He'd been hoping to set me up for Damien's death or at least to muddy the waters and deflect any focus from himself. He'd had me asking questions, chasing around to Brighton, looking like a first-rate busybody and a possible suspect to anyone who was interested. And if Nan was right, someone had been.

CHAPTER TEN

This was the world the Blitz made: claustrophobic with sudden disastrous exposures of reality and personality, followed up by tons of dust and smoke, and difficulties with my breathing apparatus. The publican, who was Wee Jimmy's uncle Alec, and I sheltered under the bar along with the few valiant customers of late afternoon while the earth shook and the air reeked with the sour smell of explosives and the rotten odor of domestic gas. "A break somewhere," said Alec, who crept out on all fours to the back room and belatedly shut off the line from the main. Clearly his ARP warden was not up to our post's standards.

A half hour later, the welcome, steady tone of the all-clear sounded. We dusted ourselves off and lifted a round to toast survival, but it was several hours before Wee Jimmy returned, bearing the usual tale of tube disruptions, detours, and stalled buses. He reported damage in the City with Spitfires in action overhead. He, himself, had been within sight of an exploding mine that "just about blew my ears off."

"A drink for the returning hero," I said. "Some of the good stuff."

His uncle glanced around to see that no one was watching, then produced a bottle of the supposedly unattainable whiskey.

"Make it a double," said Jimmy. "A man can't fight on beer."

"'*Wi' usquabae, we'll face the devil,*' as the poet says." His uncle shook his head sadly. "We're selling our birthright to the Yanks. They're taking the drink from our mouths when we're most needing a wee drop. And what are we getting for it? Rusty ships and false hopes." He filled three shot glasses.

I sipped mine, though I think perhaps you have to have a Scot somewhere in your background to enjoy even good whiskey. Wee Jimmy held his up to the light, examining it as reverently before downing it in two gulps. "Restores a man," he said. He eased onto a bar stool and leaned over confidentially. "Your nan's found a place." He handed me a slip of paper with an address on Holland Park Road. "Some old friend's the caretaker. Place is under repair but sound; I've seen it—she had me take a suitcase over for you. Try to get there before dark. The old lady may be doubtful otherwise."

I thanked him with another double and one for his uncle and made ready to go. "Can I trust anything George Frahm says?" I asked before I left.

"Such as?"

I gave them an account of George's story.

"Plenty dubious clubs in Stepney," was Wee Jimmy's opinion. "Really no other kind."

"Not many with upper rooms, though," put in his uncle.

"I need to find a bombed-out, dubious club with an upper room."

"Ah, now that would be the Brighton Arms," Alec said.

"Brighton!" Poor Connie! I hoped that he hadn't gone to seek his fortune there. And Teck came into a different light too. Could he have referred to something more than his little soirees down on the coast?

"That's right, and the fellow running it—who was that, Jimmy? A little moonfaced man with white hair and a limp."

"Found him in pieces in the street," said Jimmy. "Direct hit, mirror behind the bar shattered and took off his head. Toby. That was his name."

"Right. Toby Doodfall. Ran it with his son."

"The son survived?"

"He might have—I don't know. You'd have to ask around. Careful, mind. A rum bunch with an odd clientele, George is right about that. You could find a chief inspector and some Mayfair toff and a lad out of the alley all pigged in together, you could."

They wished me well as I left but without urging my return, which was warning enough. At Stepney Green, I found the station platforms already crowded with families, and the usual exhaust and cigarette reek was seasoned with the smell of grease, chips, and wet diapers. Harried-looking moms and dads shepherded children clutching blankets and picnic suppers, all ready to bed down as soon as the trains stopped for the night. I squeezed into the first available car, and we proceeded by fits and starts to Kensington, where the air-raid sirens were going. Though I was lucky to catch a break in the raids, it was full dark before I reached the big detached house on Holland Park Road.

I passed though a gated front garden sodden with rain and no bigger than one of my canvases, climbed the steps, and waited while the bell echoed and a misty drizzle insinuated itself down my collar and over my knees. I rang again. I was considering a host of uncomfortable options, when a shadow moved behind the door as someone had lifted a corner of the blackout shade. "It's Francis," I said, "Nan's Francis."

The shade dropped and with a rattle the door opened a fraction, then swung wide. "Come in, come in quickly."

I stepped into the darkness, the door was bolted behind me, then the overhead bulb snapped to life. I was in a wide green-tiled foyer beside a tall, slim woman with steel-gray hair and large, light, rather protuberant eyes. She wore a well-cut black dress and possessed an air of refinement, even elegance, which told me that this must be Nan's great friend Bella, about whom I had heard much and always with the added encomium that she was "the perfect nanny." Nan, of course, was the perfect nanny for me, but it was interesting to see the approved model.

"A filthy night," she said, and led me down the hall to an old-fashioned kitchen with a boarded-up window. "We had a bomb in the garden. Madame was beside herself, but I can't worry about it now. There'll be more where that one came from." She gestured for me to sit down and unwrapped two packets of sandwiches. "A nice little gift from Jessie. Your nan is always so thoughtful. And resourceful," she added with a touch of what might have been envy. "That's a nice bit of gammon."

I hoped Nan wasn't taking unnecessary risks in the provisioning department, for, yes, it was genuine gammon and very tasty. As for Bella, I could not tell from her expression how much she knew about Nan's shopping habits or whether they met with her approval; the "perfect nanny" had the face of an aging countess and the expression of a card sharp. I thought she would look wonderful at the roulette table; perhaps I could paint her there one day. Perhaps. To underline the present uncertainty, Moaning Minnie started up again. "There's a basement," Bella said, "but I don't often bother. If it's my time, it's my time."

I approved of this fatalism; we ate Nan's sandwiches and drank tea until the lights went. In the darkness, I became aware of the smell of fresh paint.

"Yes, we're redecorating. We only took minor incendiary damage but major smoke. Madame wants this floor all done over—what's the point of it now, I don't know, what with bombs every night and all the tradesmen charging the earth. I've just lost the second painter in a week. One called up—well, we can hardly complain there, can we? One got a job with the Heavy Rescue. No lamenting him, either. I hope he works harder at shoring up ruins than he did on the drawing room. I'll show you what needs to be done in the morning. Usual rates, of course. I told your nan you'd be a godsend. Madame will be over the moon with getting a painter and a decorator to boot!"

I thought I'd left fancy apartments and society décor behind, but no: I was to be painter in residence and no portraits, either. It was a good thing that we were sitting in complete darkness, because I lacked her poker face. However, by morning, kitted up in the white painter's outfit that Nan had thoughtfully packed for me, I understood the wisdom of the scheme. I was conveniently located with every excuse not to venture forth in daylight and, as a workman, well nigh invisible to any curious visitor or passerby. I consulted with Bella about the colors, agreed that my predecessor's prep work had been substandard, and broke out the brushes.

While covering the drawing room with a soft cocoa brown—trim to be an off white with a fussy gilt detail—I thought over my next move. I wasn't sure how best to track down the denizens of the late, lamented Brighton Arms. In normal times, a cruise around the area pubs and adventures combining business and pleasure would surely have turned up something. But with the whole East End pounded half to rubble; the inhabitants dead, shocked, scattered, relocated; well-heeled visitors in short supply; and the whole under a pall of toxic smoke, I felt I could delay my return to Stepney. Besides, I had several acres of inadequately prepped wall ahead of me, and I could hardly disappoint Nan's best friend.

Lulled by the monotony of broad sweeps of uninspiring color, it was noon before I considered whether I might be mistaken in regarding Brighton as either/or for Teck. *Pity, money to be made in Brighton*, he'd said. But though Teck had a place in Brighton by the sea, he had possibly indulged in London as well, and the Brighton Arms might have catered to his little theatricals. If so, despite all disclaimers, Teck might know where Connie was and maybe something about Damien, too. You can see how my imagination could "run away with me," as Nan likes to phrase it. The connection was tenuous, more than tenuous, but it was one I could follow. That night, when we again benefited from rain and cloud—discouraging, although not prohibitive, to hard-working Teutonic bombers—I set out for the Gargoyle Club. I wanted another word with my Clytemnestra.

Out of the drizzle and darkness into a dazzling burst of color and light; light broken, refracted, reflected; light prismatic, light distorted, light bouncing, light bending. And the noise: *le jazz hot,* as the French say; *le noise loud* to me; I've a tin ear. Shrieks of laughter and voices shouting from one side of the cavernous room to the other; the clicking—and occasional shattering—of glassware; drifts of smoke, from which emerged glittering dresses and real jewels and gleaming lapels, the whole atmosphere screaming *We're wild, we're gay, not even bombers can stop us.* Mild hysteria, really, but I like contrasts and here was one with a vengeance. I made my way to the bar, danced briefly with a nice chap and with his girl, too, who'd managed genuine French perfume as a riposte to Herr Hitler.

A fellow in excellent drag climbed on a table and did Vera Lynn, not half bad, either. He actually produced a few sniffles beside me with *We'll meet again, don't know where, don't know when . . .* But though I am immune to the charms of music, I took the song as an omen and hung around, hopeful, though I saw no sign of Teck. Several hours later we were hit with a heavy raid and, mindful of Jimmy's story and the mirrors everywhere, I descended with the crowd to the basement.

Someone brought a few bottles of Champagne down and, in the camaraderie of the moment, passed them 'round. Paris in the late '20s blossomed for me at the first sip. Someone began to sing in French, and out of nowhere, a clarinet started tooting. I could have been lounging in some prewar café, out for the main chance and looking to make my fortune—or at least a good dinner. Then the lights dimmed, and we felt the vibration of thunder in the earth.

When the all-clear sounded, the spell was broken. Bottles empty, the party staggered up out of the semidarkness to the brilliant mirrored rooms above. Something made me hesitate; lately, we'd all come to trust intuition, our own personal signs and superstitions. I turned and went down a couple steps to the lower landing where I saw the hair first, the shock of red, then the tall thin frame. Teck had his arm around a stout fellow's shoulders, talking confidentially as they ascended. I caught his eye and winked. He hesitated but did not stop. I expected him to visit the bar, but after a few words to his companion, Teck clapped him on the shoulder and headed for the exit. I followed.

He turned onto Dean Street, walking fast. After the bright light of the club, even the gray, cloudy night seemed very dark. Fortunately, Teck carried a shielded torch, and I caught up with him at the first new bomb crater of the evening. As we stumbled over the heaps of earth and chunks of paving, I said, "I need to talk to you."

"Not tonight. Damnation!" he exclaimed as his toe caught on some rubble.

"You don't remember me?"

"I meet so many people; absolute chaos, old boy. I can tell you there's no new productions at the moment, absolutely nothing. None, zilch, zippo. Maybe later—if the Jerries let up. But right at the moment, I don't care if you're a designer, a set painter, or a stagehand—there's no work for anyone, not unless you can dance in your skivvies at the Windmill." He giggled.

"I'm thinking of assaying Agamemnon in a private production."

"No actors, either," he began, then it registered. He stopped and raised his light briefly to my face. "What do you want?" he asked in a different tone. I detected fear. We'd gotten good at that, being now familiar with all the varieties of terror.

"I want you to look at a picture." I took his arm and drew him onto the sidewalk. "Shine your light on this." I held out Connie's photo and tried to see his face.

"No one I know. Not at all my type," he said with a touch of indignation. "Iphigenia, maybe; no possibility for Agamemnon."

I knocked the torch from his hand and grabbed him by the throat. "*You can make a lot of money in Brighton*, remember saying that? And what I want to know is did you tell this boy? Look at him."

He struggled, but though tall, he was ungainly. He stumbled back against a pile of sandbags and we both went down. I put my knee on his chest and showed him Connie's picture again.

"This is intolerable. I told you he'd be quite, quite unsuitable."

"The Brighton Arms," I said. "Fun and games on a less elevated level."

Teck made another strenuous effort to get away; I grabbed the torch and clipped him one. A thick ribbon of blood slid from his nose and suddenly he was a good deal more amenable. "I could get you work," he said in a quick, breathless voice. "A private job for me. Maybe Brighton again, what about that? You can let me up now, we'll work something out."

"I'll break your neck," I said. "I want to know where this boy is and what you told him about Brighton."

"The best Agamemnon, really; you were the very best."

I hit him again. As I say, the war had unsettled us all. "Listen," I said, "that was pleasure, this is business. Look again."

Teck twitched and wriggled then let his head drop onto the sandbags and tried to staunch his nose with his handkerchief. "I might have done," he said.

"Done what?" I clutched the front of his shirt. "What?"

"Told him about Brighton, the club. I only take very special people to my little pied-à-terre at the shore."

"Why did he want to know? What was he looking for?"

"How should I know that? Who knows what's in anybody's mind, far less some street boy's."

"You'd better think," I said, raising the flashlight. I really believe I would have done him harm if he hadn't found his tongue.

"Something about his mate, this Damien somebody. He'd been found dead in the park. I don't know what that had to do with the Brighton Arms, but it had nothing to do with me; I'm not that type at all—finesse and fake knives and once in a while a blunt razor. The merest scratch suffices. You know all about that!"

"Go on."

"Nothing, just we got talking one night. And he was on about this Damien boy."

"Where was this?"

"The Pond—a frightful dive, not my usual sort of place. He was just part of the local color, you understand. I bought him a drink. He said he wasn't afraid of anything if the money was good. That's what he said."

"And you sent him there—you knew the size of him! What do you suppose happened to him?"

"Nothing, for all I know. The Blitz started and the place was hit early on by the wrath of God; there's nothing but glass and dust left."

"So where is he now?"

"I don't know. He might have died in the Blitz. Honestly. I think he did go to the shore, though. I think he did. No, no," he said as I raised the torch. "Last time I saw him, I mentioned I hadn't seen him at the Arms. And he said that he'd looked into it. That's exactly how he phrased it, and he said that he was going out of town for a while. 'I'm off to entertain the troops' was how he put it." Teck giggled again.

"Could those two things be related?"

"I don't know. Could be he earned a few pounds. Could be he met someone he wanted to stay clear of. I don't think you need worry about him."

"Why's that?"

"He was a tough little bastard. He told me that anyone who hurt him was going to be sorry—and I believed him."

CHAPTER ELEVEN

I returned so late it was useless to attempt the house. In her perfect nanny voice, Bella had given me to understand that the place would be locked up tight by ten. Fortunately the little front gate was open. I made my way to the back, forced the door of the garden shed, and caught a couple hours' sleep amid bales of peat moss, stacks of terra-cotta pots, various canisters of fertilizer and insecticides, and a peasant arsenal of hoes, cultivators, scythes, and spades. I bedded down on some old burlap sacks as the all-clear sounded, and I was up to ring the bell at nine. Nan's friend opened the door with an approving glance at her watch.

After a pot of strong tea and some very presentable scones, I resumed work on the drawing room. This was the pattern of the next few days: toiling in the decorating vineyards before and after lunch, the occasional phone call from Nan providing a welcome break midafternoon, then out on the town amid raids and alarms to look for anyone who knew Connie or the Brighton Arms crowd. A crazy life, really. Once in a while, ignoring the risk presented by my former ARP colleagues, I visited the old Chelsea Church where Arnold was a fire watcher.

My situation improved when I was at last entrusted with a door key, partly on the grounds of my model behavior and quick progress on the decorating front, partly because "Madame would never approve of anyone sleeping in the garden shed." *Merci beaucoup*, Madame. I now had a proper bed under the eaves, where, on early nights in, I sometimes heard incendiaries rattling down the slates. Bella and I extinguished a couple in the garden with a big bucket of sand, and, for this service, I moved into high favor. I might, I suppose, have kept my head down and bunked there indefinitely; the house was a large one, and on close examination all the walls needed work. If I'd only had canvases and an easel, I might have been quite content covering Madame's walls in the murky shades she favored.

Instead, I sought the bright lights, metaphorically speaking—all the theater marquees were dark and the restaurants swathed in blackout curtains. I wandered up and down the pitchy streets of Soho, drinking with likely boys and chatting up prosperous steamers in the hopes of Champagne. I heard a variety of tales about the old Brighton Arms, as well as highly colored accounts of its flaming demise. Some remembered a chap who resembled my inspector; most did not, and I decided he could not have been a regular. Perhaps George was correct, but more likely he had chosen to deflect attention from himself by spreading rumors about Mordren.

Teck was another matter. Arnold had a useful friend employed at the *Daily Telegraph*, and a trip to their morgue had secured me photos of both my inspector and Teck. Perhaps it was his distinctive hair or his obsession with Clytemnestra, but the easily recognizable Teck had made an impression on half the boys of Soho; "completely potty" was the consensus.

"Violent, do you think?"

"Well, that was the stock in trade, wasn't it? You went there to get knocked around or to knock around." My informant was a wiry boy with black hair and a beaky nose over a sadly receding chin. “But more theatrical, that’s what he was. He liked a good deal of screaming but he wasn’t keen on damage.”

That was my impression. On the more important question of poor Damien—and also on the character of George Frahm—all were silent. The most that would be said was that the Brighton Arms was very discreet and the management heavy handed. It didn’t do to talk about their clientele or, as one boy put it, to complain of bumps and bruises. I wondered if that had been Damien’s mistake or if he’d contemplated a little not-so-discreet blackmail. There were so many possibilities with such an outfit that only my love of sex and drink kept me hard at work.

One night when the docks were being pulverized and the sky was full of fire and thunder, I decided to risk The Pond. Having seen the inspector there at the start of the whole miserable business, I’d been giving it a wide berth, but Connie had been a regular, and I’d turned up very little on him elsewhere. As I left the tube station, I stuck my tin hat on my head and tried to look purposeful. Sirens and fire engines and the rattle of ack-ack guns; oily water underfoot, sky red around the horizon, the zenith black overhead but lit with extraordinary white fireworks like giant flaming candelabras, the whole crossed by searchlights: altogether an amazing effect. Down on ground level mesmerizing blocks of flame were shooting enough heat and draft to knock a man over. I was enlisted to help one weary fireman with a hose—the rest of his squad having wandered off for a pint—and with that and the smoke and dust in the air, I was dirty enough to pass as an active-duty warden by the time I pushed through the blackout curtain and entered the pub.

Was my inspector there? In my imagination, he’d been roosting at The Pond bar ever since I’d made my escape from the museum, and I glanced around nervously as dull booms in the distance set the pyramids of glassware on the bar jittering and rattling. No, no, I was safe for the moment; my rampant imagination, formerly tethered to my easel, had again deceived me: the inspector had more pressing work than staking out a club in hopes of catching me.

I ordered wine, prompted by nostalgia rather than any hope of real vintage, and I was checking out the room—painted faces, polished nails, lots of khaki and blue sprinkled with a few of the gruff and tweed-coated—when a tall man with short cropped hair and a taut, strained face appeared at my elbow. Something military once, I guessed, correctly, for he was missing a hand, and when he turned full I could see the burn scars down the left side of his face. A pilot, probably, though Dunkirk and points east were certainly possibilities.

We started to talk, and, by force of habit, I brought the conversation 'round to Connie. By then I'd perfected my spiel. I owed him a couple of quid for delivering paintings and couldn't seem to get in touch.

"Connie?"

"Colin Williams." I fished the picture from my pocket. "Connie in his leisure hours."

"Better try Miss Cherie now," he said.

I was ready to pass on to other topics when a bell rang: the business cards and flyers of the enterprising Miss Cherie of Brighton. I had to buy my companion a couple of drinks to get the rest, but sure enough, he did know Connie, had known him first at The Pond. "A good mate in a fight," he said rather surprisingly. "Shows you can't always go by appearances. There he was flouncing around, forever weeping over a boyfriend and fussing with his mascara."

"That's our Connie," I said.

"A tough little bugger, nonetheless. We were in this bar once and, well, I was drunk enough to forget I was missing my left. That was just after. Bought it in a training accident," he said with a touch of bitterness. "I never got within sight of the Jerries."

I sympathized as best I could though the military mind remains a closed book to me.

"I'd have been in difficulties without our friend. He smashed a bottle and went for the fellow; blood on the bar, I can tell you. We had quite a song and dance about it, but since I'd lost a hand for king and country—" He nodded his head and added, "I've had a soft spot for Connie ever since."

"He really did go to Brighton, then? I mean, Miss Cherie?"

"Yes, that fight was in Brighton as a matter of fact, and he was Miss Cherie then. I recognized him, of course, though he was pretty good—very good really. First glance or under the influence, ninety percent would have been fooled. Gave me a wink, he did, and I said, 'Can we dance, miss?'"

"Did he tell you why he'd left London?"

"He said he was making a killing. Broadening his clientele. But I think there was something more, because he seemed jumpy and nervous. He said being Miss Cherie all the time took the fun out of it."

"Why do you suppose . . . ?"

"Usual reason. Somebody behind him, I'd guess. Could be you for all I know." His eyes were chilly with the remote expression I'd noticed pilots acquired—or cultivated.

"I thought it might have been someone from the Brighton Arms."

"The Brighton Arms is long gone. But you've been asking around about him."

Clearly my inquiries had preceded me. "I owe him money. I like to pay my debts."

"A rarity in this naughty world." He sounded unconvinced but perhaps the Brighton Arms was a taboo topic, for he immediately began a conversation with a plump chap in an expensive suit and an ill-fitting wig. I left soon afterward, sat out an intense raid in a tube station, and snuck into the Old Chelsea Church in time to tell Arnold the latest intelligence.

"I can get Connie's number," he said, "if those cards and flyers are still around. No, no trouble. You remember the doorman?"

I did.

"I'll call him tomorrow; he's willing to be obliging."

I hugged him. Arnold is so reliable and sensible, plus practical like Nan. I said I'd finish his shift with him and we let his usual fire-watching partner go home. Ah, romantic evenings on the edge of the inferno! From the spire, the fires of London seethed gold and crimson like the poet's lakes in hell, but inside the spire—well, there was paradise. Nothing like contrast, I say.

Arnold was as good as his word. Nan phoned me the next afternoon, interrupting a swath of dull maroon—a deadening color, and in the dining room of all places—with the number. I went straight to the nearest phone box and dialed.

A great clinking of pennies, the clunk as the machine digested them, the furry sound of the line, the distant ringing, then a woman's voice repeated the number I had reached.

"Could I speak to Miss Cherie, please?"

A burst of profanity and the line went dead. I tried twice more, before, in a moment of inspiration, I introduced myself as Police Inspector Mordren. Miss Cherie, aka Collin Williams, was—I cast about for what might sound impressive—"a material witness in a very serious case."

More linguistic fireworks. "I've got a serious enough case right here, I can assure you. She's skipped out on a month's rent, and her pulling in pounds every night. Pounds, the disgraceful hussy."

"When was this?"

"Last week. She's been gone a full week, and there's me keeping the room for her and going without the rent. I'm a widow, I am." She had a good line in this vein. Each time the pips started I frantically stuffed coins into the ravenous phone box. I did learn that it hadn't been unusual for Miss Cherie to be away for days at a time. "You can guess what she was up to."

I thought I could, as a matter of fact. "Did she give any indication she was coming back?"

"Every indication! Do you think I'd have let her out of the house with a case otherwise? I wasn't found yesterday in the cabbage patch, you know."

I asked if she had any idea where the disgraceful hussy might have gone.

"London, and good riddance, I am sure. If one of the bombs gets her, it's no more than she deserves. What I'm to do for the rent is beyond me. You find her, you see she sends me seven and six." She elaborated on this until the pips again sounded and I hung up, feeling slightly more sympathetic to my inspector. I'd spent four days in concentrated effort and all I could be sure of was that Connie hadn't met a bad end at the Brighton Arms. I should have been happy about that, but I was vaguely dissatisfied. If Connie had returned to London, why hadn't I run across him in one of his old haunts?

Perhaps his landlady was wrong. Perhaps he had headed for parts unknown or met disaster in Brighton. Perhaps he's even now floating out to sea or rotting under the pier. *Somebody behind him*, my crippled informant had said. Somebody from Brighton? No, logically, someone from London who might have followed him to Brighton. I began to feel more suspicious of Teck again. It was funny. Suspicion had a way of evaporating in his presence and regrouping in his absence. But then he was a man of the theatre. Just because he was a lousy Clytemnestra didn't mean he wasn't able to act a part. I thought I'd very much like to follow him around London, and the next night, I set out for the Gargoyle again.

CHAPTER TWELVE

I had no luck for several nights, and I began to fear that Teck had returned to Brighton and his Greek theatricals. Then, on Thursday, I finished up the dining-room trim early in the afternoon. The next project was the foyer, featuring a curving formal staircase with a twenty-foot ceiling over the stairwell. I told Bella that I wouldn't attempt it without scaffolding, and, with every bit of pipe, plank, and scaffolding going for essential repairs, it looked to be some time before I could resume work. Bella paid me for the two rooms completed, and I promised myself dinner in Soho.

I smartened up my appearance as best I could—Nan, god bless her, is resistant to the charms of makeup—borrowed a torch from Bella, and ventured out into fog with drizzle, the best kind of weather for the new dispensation. If the tide was in, the firemen would have an easy time on the pumps tonight, and with the heavy cloud cover, we might get a break. Might or might not—the sirens were going when I emerged at Leicester Square, and I ducked back inside. Waves of bombers rumbled overhead, the sound of their engines shaking the earth, but their payloads had been farther east, and when I emerged into the gray twilight, there were only the normal quotient of fires, a scattering of white hot incendiaries, and a single massive crater that was tying up the buses and forcing the fire engines and ambulances onto the sidewalks and down alleys. A fine nuisance, but we'd lost the panic of early days: dust and smoke and sudden death were just the way of the world. I had money in my pocket and fancied a French meal.

I was running through a variety of menus—mostly wishful thinking—when I spotted Teck. There was no mistaking the tall, angular figure, the dreadful hair, or the curious gliding walk that hinted Clytemnestra lurked in some obscure wing of his psyche. I turned on my heel and trailed him to the tube station where, amid the crowd of passengers and shelterers, I managed to follow him through the passages of the Embankment station to the District Line. When he took the eastbound train, I figured Stepney, and although I lost sight of him several times, I hopped out confidently at Stepney Green.

No Aubrey Teck. Platform jammed, of course: the poor lack gardens with Anderson shelters, and even if they'd had them, the district had been hit so hard that few gardens were left. Could he have slipped out at Whitechapel or ridden on to Bow Road? I'd had my eyes peeled at all the earlier stations, but in the crush anything was possible. Go on? Go back? I was hesitating between the exit and the train when I saw him far down the platform. He had gotten into an altercation with an old fellow carrying an accordion for tonight's entertainment in the Underground. I dodged into the exit tunnel and up to the street. Five minutes later, half hidden by a bulwark of sandbags, I saw him emerge from the station and head east.

I had been in the area only recently with Wee Jimmy, but already the physical landscape was quite altered. The usual fire watchers and wardens were about, along with ambulances, bomb disposal trucks, auxiliary fire equipment, and rescue workers. Moving among them, I missed my tin hat and badge, my passport to the night, my stamp of legitimacy. Along the side streets, dubious types readied for *their* night's work—looting was lucrative, especially when big shops and nightclubs were hit. The alcoholic, homeless, and bomb-shattered drifted aimlessly until corralled by the wardens, who urged them into the Underground or one of the public shelters. A cloak of mist and smoke swirled over all this misery, but fortunately Teck kept his torch lit. I switched my own off and followed his yellow point of light as closely as I dared.

We passed into a warren of cramped tenements and small shops, all shuttered and boarded, some badly damaged, mere hulks. I was struck by how swiftly and confidently Teck moved; clearly he was no stranger. And though now that I thought of it, there was a hint of Cockney under his theatrical English, the district changed so quickly that he must come here often. After stumbling for the third or fourth time, I was sorry that I couldn't say the same. I was dusting myself off and checking for damage when I realized all was dark ahead. I ran forward, seeking an alley or a doorway, and banged into a protective hurdle. My heart jumping, I switched on my torch. The light shot into a bomb crater fifteen or twenty feet deep with water at the bottom. Not a cheering sight for a non-swimmer.

Had Teck turned off somewhere unseen, or had he known of the obstacle and hoped anyone following him would not? Unpleasant prospects all 'round. I switched off my torch to let my eyes adjust. The street had taken a direct hit, and I was facing a rubble-filled lot with no lights anywhere. Then I noticed what appeared to be warehouses across the wasteland and a brief flicker of light like the opening of a door. I waited several minutes before picking my way around the bomb site. When I reached the block, I found most of the buildings shuttered tight, but faint sounds of music—rhythmic, American, jazzy—issued from behind one otherwise-anonymous door. I knocked but got no answer, and, after scouting around to be sure there was no other entrance, I had resigned myself to waiting for Teck to emerge when a pair of torches approached, carried by two heavy, prosperous-looking chaps. They were laughing in a knowing but nervous way, and I heard one say he could smell tea burning, and the other that danger is the spice of life.

They went straight to the door and instead of knocking began fumbling with their keys. "Evening," I said. "I'm in luck."

They froze.

"Forgot my key. Damnable nuisance. A night like this a man needs some distraction."

"You're not a member." It always amazes me how clubmen scent one another, as if membership came with some sharp new aroma. He swung his light insolently into my face.

"Well, not yet, but George thought I'd do."

"George?"

I thought perhaps I'd made a mistake, but no. Another close inspection of my features.

"You might do indeed." This from the taller of the two. He had a shock of white hair and a red face with a massive nose and pursed lips.

There was no mistaking the slightly flirtatious tone.

"George is never wrong, is he?"

The hitherto silent one, dapper in a touring cap and an ascot, started to giggle. George's infallibility seemed a great joke. "George will break your neck if you're lying about him," said the first man.

"Or *to* him," said the second, and giggled again. A man who's so jovial in the Blitz is either drunk or a psychopath.

"George is a special taste," I said, and this time they both laughed. The first man stuck his key in the lock and gestured me to follow them inside.

Excellent blackout preparation, that was the first thing. I approved; this ARP warden will give them a commendation. If you're going into the lion's den, so to speak, you don't want to be hit by some sharp-eyed Jerry cruising at ten thousand feet—such double jeopardy seems quite unfair. Very dim lighting for another thing, excellent in my opinion. I don't know that I'd have spotted George if he'd been three feet from me, and I figured Teck would have as hard a time picking me out. And then the bar: large and well stocked, though the room itself showed signs of bomb damage in the residual tarpaulins and bracing. I decided to let one of my randy and well-to-do acquaintances buy me some champers and see what developed. They looked a bit soft and easy for my taste, but careful, Francis! Danger is so seductive I find it easy to slide from business to pleasure. I drank some bad bubbly and allowed the genuine clubmen certain liberties before I said that I should find George. "I know you think I'm dubious."

"I know you are," one said, giggling. "I only like dubious boys."

We had something in common there!

The big, red-faced chap was very keen to "adjourn," as he put it, to somewhere private, but though that might be amusing, I already knew as much as I needed to know about him.

"I'd better see George. You know what he's like."

Oh, yes, he did, he did. A vigorous nodding of his heavy head. I mistrust a man who retains jowls during rationing. He had a face like a side of beef, and my hand twitched for a brush: cad red and white lead with a touch of ochre; dark underneath, purples and umbers like the darkness of the soul. One big swirl for his nose; the paint pulled into folds, and folds rippling into flesh. I saw it in an instant, then caught myself: to dream here with dragons all around was dangerous. "Where am I likely to find him?"

"Up the stair." He pointed into the distant reaches of the club, over the dancers, the crowded bar, the couples locked in frantic embraces in the booths. "'Come back with your shield or on it!'"

Another poof besotted with the classics. I wiggled my ass at him and made my way through the throng of punters and painted boys, many with bruised faces or cut lips. Oh, this was a select and special clientele, one doubtless made in heaven for my friend George, whom I hoped, at all cost, to avoid. Up the stair, rickety, I noted; I was becoming, thanks to my ARP training, a bit of an old woman as far as safety went. Down a corridor, lighting also not up to any known code; this must once have been part of the storerooms. Closed doors on either side emitted noises of pleasure and pain: the delightful sounds of extreme emotion. Steady on, Francis! To be dutiful, as Nan says, is sometimes a virtue. Dear Nan, with her inflexible manners and flexible morals.

I suspected that Teck was not thus engaged. How did I know? I didn't, but Blitz life was such a lottery that hesitation was a chief danger. I was surprised that "Dithering Costs Lives" had not joined "Be Like Dad, Keep Mum" or "Go by Shank's Pony" and the various injunctions against waste and in favor of a cabbage-based cuisine.

Various empty rooms. I checked one out: a bed, a chair, a washstand, a little cupboard with a nice line of whips, a few badly done pornographic pictures on the wall. I suspect sex will become my subject, but, the Muse willing, nothing so unimaginative as these. It's the emotions of the act I'm interested in; the rest is just the collision of so much meat. We are flesh, and there's the end of the matter. Anyone who's worked a bomb site knows that.

Another stair; our masters choose to live on high. I started up, soft-footed, to what I guessed had been the original warehouse offices. Voices above, but no pleasurable pains here. And no theatrical English, either. Stress had sent Teck's plummy vowels all to hell.

" . . . a crap position. I thought he was going to beat my head in."

A baritone rumble. He was keeping his voice down admirably.

"You said you'd take care of it before!"

A threatening sound; in a dog, it would be a growl. The human equivalent was at once softer and nastier. I moved several steps closer. The door above was closed, but age and blasts had disturbed the casement so that a broad, uneven sweep of light issued over the sill.

"It wasn't enough, though, was it? And the park! The park, of all places."

"Weren't bomb craters then, were there? A man can disappear now, and if he's found at all, the Jerries take the blame. It's a great time for my line of work."

"That may be all right for you, but a man in my position—"

I recognized the sound of bodies colliding; George had a low flashpoint and a very low opinion of Teck's "position."

The designer showed more pluck than I'd expected. "All right, all right," he said. "Remember what pays the bills. You hired him, it was your mess, and you didn't clean it up. But water over the dam; no more said. Now there's another problem, that's all I'm saying."

"Yeah? And the other one? The little blonde? Whose idea was that?"

"He seemed a good sort of lad—"

"You wouldn't smell a rat until he shat on your shoe."

"If you hadn't flown off the handle. I warned . . . "

The other speaker did not wait to answer this observation. "Not to mention your other little problem. What raised questions in the first place but your fucking play acting?"

" . . . you, but no, no. You'd do it your way, heavy handed . . . "

I heard the clatter of a chair going over; George clearly believed in his own infallibility. But was it George—or was memory deceiving me? At the moment, for reasons I cannot now recall or imagine, it seemed important to know for sure. I climbed the rest of the way, my heart jumping with each creak of the treads and peered into the semidarkness. I was in a sort of attic, one part finished—the office where Teck was having his conference—the other a sort of lumber room. As I picked my way over some dusty boxes, I felt the familiar tickle in the back of my throat, followed by a nasty rattling wheeze. I stopped mid-stride and looked around for cover. The voices in the other room were silent.

"You've just got the wind up," Teck said in a nasty voice.

I felt as if I was suffocating. Underfoot was an assortment of old boxes; cases of empty bottles, a few loose; treacherous bits of glassware; pieces of wood; bales of what appeared to be rags as well as chairs and other household items all jumbled together like a decayed pawnshop. There was barely enough light for me to see my way, but once the office door opened, I would be exposed in more ways than one. Back over the boxes and crackling bits of dry leather—whatever were those?—before the sharp crunch of breaking glass, loud as a gunshot. I lunged for the stair and, half running, half falling, clattered to the bottom as the door opened.

A shout above; I raced down the corridor, slid into that empty, ill-appointed room, and fumbled for the lock. No such luck, just a little slide bolt for privacy, the sort rendered useless with a good kick. Teck and his associate were in the hall; I braced myself against the door, my chest heaving, my breath coming like a bellows. I was on the verge of a full-blown asthma attack, when the Muse who looks out for the wayward and foolish brought inspiration. I groaned loudly. Another great wheeze, followed, despite my Sahara mouth, by a burst of salacious profanity. Another groan, ending in gasps: *yes, yes, yes!* Realistic? You bet. I felt as if my lungs would absolutely collapse.

Footsteps in the hall and muffled curses from the man I believed was George. "Someone up to no good."

"One of the fucking punters," was Teck's opinion. "Up for a free show. Can't trust them."

I was panting like a steam engine.

"We'll have a good look downstairs," said George. "You're too damn careless."

"Look who's talking."

Bodies colliding again; Teck was a slow learner. When the sound of their footsteps faded, I slid the bolt, gasping, and glanced into the hall in time to see George's gorilla back and fine black hair. I closed the door and sat down on the floor, a major error: dust between the old boards, dust lurking in the baseboard, dust, no doubt, between the sheets and under the bed, dust containing—for all I knew—essence of dog, the worst of all possible dusts. I staggered to the small window and thrust it open, forgetting, in my anxiety, that the night air held pulverized London and the smoke of flaming petrol. My vision went black for an instant; when the night returned to focus, I was swaying out of the window like a sailor on a bender. I grabbed the casement and hauled myself back, then sat down on the bed and tried to bring my breath into order.

While I was still gasping, the Muse, my friend and enemy, offered up the realization that Teck and George, having gone downstairs, had left their office empty. I eased the door and hustled for the stair. Simple this time; they'd left the door open and the light on, which meant that they would return shortly. Hurry up, Francis! Inside: desk with whiskey bottle on top. I overcame my dislike of the malt and took a good swig for my straining bronchi. Next, file cabinets with helpful alphabetical labels. What had we here? I went straight to *M*—*M* for Mordren, *M* for my inspector, *M* for a folder with a strip of film and an envelope of black-and-white photos and negatives, very grainy and of execrable composition but revealing, truly revealing. I stuck both in my jacket pocket.

Though I was seriously tempted to explore further, I descended, checked the hallway, and after several deep breaths—thank you, George, for that little stimulant—went down to the club as boldly as I could. I considered whistling but rejected that touch as over the top. Down, down the open stair into the fog of smoke and perfume and male secretions; I swam through the throng, passed the bar, was within a step of the door with my hand on the blackout curtain when George let out his primeval roar. I lunged through the curtain to grab the doorknob. Locked? Was it locked? Dreadful safety arrangements—especially for me. A latch, perhaps? I touched something, turned it, grasped the knob again, thrust with all my weight and practically fell outside. I scrambled to my feet and ran into the darkness. That is, I lifted my feet and put them down, but there was so little air in my lungs that I was barely trotting, never mind running. They caught me before I reached the first alley.

Teck had a light and George brought his fists. When I tried to evade both, we all three wound up in the road.

"Get him out of the street!" shouted Teck. "Take him inside."

I wasn't keen on that and struck out wildly, connecting with George at least once. He performed considerably better, and once he had me on the ground, he commenced kicking with his customary enthusiasm while Teck, with some remnant of bourgeois propriety, screamed for a change of venue. I felt blood in my mouth and pain in my kidneys as I struggled to protect my head and trip George. I was doing poorly at both when a siren shrieked in the night. I saw the shielded lights of an oncoming ambulance and heard the shouts of the driver. Teck and

George dove for the sidewalk and, terrified, I flattened myself against the tarmac. The high vehicle passed over me with a roar, then skidded to a stop, brakes squealing. Purely on instinct, I got to my feet. In the momentary confusion of the shouting ambulance men and the raucous replies of my tormentors, I plunged into the rubble field and scrambled, wheezing and half conscious, over fallen walls and beams, toilets and washstands, bits of pipe, shattered casements, and broken doors. Bricks slipped away underfoot and rattled into unseen voids and caverns. They would be right behind me, and my only thought was to find a hiding place until I could breathe enough to run.

Fear carried me almost across the lot before the siren howled again and the angry voices resumed outside of the club. Teck had a light, and both he and George knew the area. The conviction that they'd know where I had gone sent me floundering forward. Almost at once the ground shifted under my feet and sent me sliding willy-nilly. I clawed at the rubble, tearing my hands on sharp bits of metal and collecting splinters everywhere but to no avail; my footing was lost, I began a terrible downward acceleration and landed with a splash in utter darkness.

CHAPTER THIRTEEN

Complete panic. Splashing, flailing, water up my nose, down my throat, lungs in rebellion, death a near certainty. I'd have shouted for George if my voice had been more than a croak. Struggling to keep my head above water, I flapped my arms and kicked my feet until I felt a sharp pain in my left hand. Automatically, I thrust my arm above water and stood up. I was in hip-deep liquid, cold, undoubtedly filthy, but shallow. I was saved. Now a revulsion for the muddy water, for mysterious objects soft and sharp, for the crater, overcame me. My first thought was to risk everything and climb out. My second was for the photos. Patting my jacket, I found the film and the envelope, damp but intact despite the best efforts of George and the Luftwaffe. This was my real salvation—and Nan's, too—if I could just get the goods out of Stepney.

Out, that was the thing, but not yet, Francis! And better hope that neither George nor Teck had heard me floundering across the puddle. With a sudden liquid ripple, something moved at the very edge of my vision: a rat, more than one. I couldn't leave the crater, not yet, but getting out of the water was definitely on the program. I felt around the edge with my uninjured hand, seeking a timber, a bit of a table or a door, a solid chunk of masonry, all the while listening for footsteps and voices among the intermittent sounds of sirens, motors, and planes.

I touched what felt like part of a wall, got a grip on the edge, scraped my knees and knocked my shins, but managed, with a nasty sucking sound, to leave the mud and water of the pit. A rustle down in the porous depths below sent me scrambling higher, only to lose purchase and slide halfway back. In the dark it was hard to judge which handholds in the debris might be trusted and which, loose or crumbling, would shoot me back into the water.

I had clambered a fair way up the steep and treacherous slope when I heard approaching steps—not the scramble and rattle of a passage across the rubble but the steady, respectable tread of the street. I was about to shout for help when a round beam of light touched the top of the crater and ran along the edge. I was squatting beside a slab of lath and plaster, and I squeezed against this frail protection. The light roamed down the slope across from me, pausing at any hollow or projection, then continued on its way. Someone searching, perhaps for me.

"Hopeless," said a voice. It was Teck, and I was thankful I'd kept quiet.

"Many lives as a bloody cat. He should have been killed by the ambulance."

"How deep's the water?"

A few seconds of silence, then a hollow splash below. I hoped it sounded deep enough so that they would not think to explore the near side, where I was hidden in shadow.

"He'll float by morning," said George. "See you check."

"Check yourself." There was some disagreement about this before their footsteps faded under the drone of the planes and the distant rattle of the guns. My impulse was to get myself over the top and away, but I crouched shivering, teeth chattering for what seemed to be hours, listening to the raids and watching the fire glow from the burning docks. At last, a lull overhead, and half frozen, I attacked the last dozen feet of the slope, slipped and failed once, twice, three times, managed most of the way on the fourth, and, finally, nearly exhausted and covered in bruises and dirt, clawed my way to the top and the protective hurdle at the edge of the road.

I pulled myself upright and staggered off in such a state that I'm not sure I'd have made it home if an ambulance crew returning empty had not spotted me. I was so dirty that they assumed I'd been in a blast, and they kept asking where I lived and when we'd been hit. I feigned concussion, which was not terribly difficult under the circumstances. They took me to a busy Whitechapel dressing station, where a strapping volunteer nurse with a loud voice and a good line of reassuring chatter poured disinfectant on my cuts and stitched up my hand. I fell asleep on the floor, surrounded by sobbing children, moaning adults, and the general chaos of the hurt and newly homeless. At dawn I got directions to the tube station and, disregarding medical advice, my filthy and bedraggled state, and the benefits of my hideout on Holland Park Road, made my way home to Nan.

Even with her short sight, she could see I'd been in the wars. "Dear boy! Whatever's happened?"

I reassured her as best I could while she busied herself with ridding me of my filthy garments and bundling me up in a dressing gown and blanket. This revealed the extent of my personal damage. Of course, the dressing station's efforts were not up to her standard, and, in fact, they had missed some nasty splinters in my thigh. Nan got out her big magnifying glass and a needle and went to work while I drank scalding tea with honey and a little whiskey—Nan's sworn remedy—and recounted my adventures in the bomb crater. She extracted a particularly dirty-looking piece of wood and was daubing the wound with peroxide when I remembered my treasure lying on the floor with my unceremoniously discarded jacket.

Nan ran her glass over the images, shook her head at the ways of the world, then nodded. "You did very well, dear boy. But at what cost!"

"Nothing was planned; it was all was spur of the moment." I took her magnifying glass and studied the images. No sign of Damien, but any pictures of him in action would surely be long gone. Even reckless George would not have risked that. But that he and Teck were running a blackmail operation was beyond doubt. Indeed, blackmail might have been the real raison d'être for the Brighton Arms and its present incarnation. I guessed that Damien, discovering their venture, had attempted to turn it to his own account. Maybe he'd pinched some of the evidence; my own experience suggested there would have been opportunities. Had he tried to blackmail the supposedly respectable Teck or one of the other clients and gotten murdered for his pains? Or had George discovered the theft and settled the matter in his own inimitable way? Either way, the material in my hand raised questions about the inspector, who might have limited his investigation or tried to set me up even if he, himself, were innocent of the killing.

"Will someone be looking for these?"

"I doubt they realize I've got them, though they might look for me anyway. They don't know where I live, and I don't think they know my name, but as you see, they have police connections. I'm hoping they think I'm dead."

"Don't rely on hopes," said Nan. "Let me see if I can dry these, and you return to Bella."

I didn't like that idea at all, but Nan was insistent, and I'd have been out of the flat and gone if I hadn't nearly fallen off the chair, shivering. Nan got another blanket, thinking I was chilled, but when I told her both my head and my hand were throbbing, she looked grave.

"It's just the stitching," I said, hopeful.

She inspected the wound with her glass again and had me do the same. "Did it bleed well?"

I said it had.

"That's good—best way to wash the wound. We'll need to watch it, though. Anything could have been in that water."

"Anything was," I assured her. She brought me another cup of strong tea with half the week's ration of sugar and another generous tot of whiskey and had me go to bed. I lay there shaking for some time before I fell into dreams of dark, under-scaled rooms where I struggled to stand erect and of vast alleys floored in water like the canals of Venice. It was night when I woke, my mouth dry, my hand only moderately sore, and everything else at least provisionally operational. I had no idea of the time, but before I could put on the light, I realized the sirens were going. A moment later, Nan came in. "You're awake."

"I'm a bit better."

"We should go to the basement. This is the second wave; it looks like a bad night."

I'd slept through the first lot; how adaptable we are. I got up, shaky from lack of food, and followed her through the flat. We'd lost power, but though I had to feel my way, Nan moved confidently, indifferent to the darkness, not even thinking of a torch: further confirmation that her sight was seriously eroded. As we went through the kitchen and out to the basement steps, I remarked that I didn't hear the girls from upstairs.

"They're at the ministry. The office workers sleep there most nights now. They'll be back, one of them at least, for an hour or two during the day to pick up clothes."

"You're alone then, Nan." I didn't like that at all. Especially now.

"The butcher comes in if he's working late. 'Any port in a storm,' he says."

I struck a match and located a couple of the old mildewed chairs stored below. The light flared and went out, leaving a sulfur smell and pitch-darkness. Dampness tickled the back of my throat, and I began wheezing softly. "Though," said Nan, after a moment, "I've had the strangest sense lately."

A pause in which I remembered the stories she used to tell me; the ghost stories of old dark houses where one met sinister inhabitants or where strange visitors came to call, stories where worlds were permeable and the unseen was just on the other side of a wall. "Yes?"

"Of someone being here. Someone else. It started just after you went to Bella's. A couple of times I've been so sure I could hear someone breathing. There's nothing wrong with my ears, you know."

I agreed with that. Nan's hearing has always been acute.

"But even without a sound, sometimes you just know there's some—presence."

"A ghostly visitor?" I asked, half joking.

"I don't think so. Someone without a torch. Who goes without one?"

"Well, we're down here without," I said.

"Only because you keep losing your light. I hope that wasn't one of Bella's."

I had to admit it was. "You didn't hear anyone come in, though?"

"Someone was already here. I thought first it was one of the girls, but you know how friendly they are. I called for them. No answer. I was at the doorway, and I turned around and went up. If I'd had the key, I'd have locked the door behind me and seen what was what in the morning."

"See you notify the police if it happens again," I said. "Don't you go exploring on your own."

"Look who's talking. And then last night—well, no matter now," she said and patted my uninjured hand.

"No, tell me. We have to stay alert. Especially now. You did dry those photos?" I asked. Despite marked improvement, I realized that my mind had lost sequence as well as time.

"Cleaned up and drying in the airing cupboard."

"That's our insurance policy, Nan."

"I'll guard them with my life."

"So last night—"

"I was here on my own. A light on proper, all in order, not a bad raid—I'd have stayed upstairs but for promising you. I heard someone on the stair. And I don't know why, but it gave me a turn—with it being too late for the butcher and with the girls sleeping in the City. I reached up and put off the light."

"And then?"

"Someone came to the door, opened it. I could just see the night, the fire in the clouds. Someone was there and stepped in without a greeting. Since when do you do that! I didn't say a thing. Not a peep.

No torch again this time. Closed the door. I could hear the footsteps. All quiet. I was about to turn the light on again when I heard someone walking overhead. All through the flat and then out."

"Was anything missing? What did he want?"

"You'll need to tell me if there's anything gone, dear boy, but I can tell you, *he* didn't want anything, for it was a woman. I could hear the tap of the high heels. What do you think of that?"

I should have thought a lot about it, but just then the vague rumblings of my intestinal tract and the faint queasiness of my stomach increased to violent intensity. I lunged for the door, tripped, and gagged and would have fouled the basement if Nan hadn't opened the door and guided me up to the back garden where I retched up a lot of nasty fluid in the pink-and-gray raid light. A moment or two later, I had to struggle into the flat to the WC, where I spent a good deal of time expelling the varied toxins I'd picked up in the water. By the time I staggered out to be dosed again with whiskey-laced tea, I had only one thought: to sleep.

CHAPTER FOURTEEN

I lost three days with fever and intestinal grief. Nan must have begged sugar from half the street, for every time I awakened, I got sweet tea with whiskey or lemon—another rarity. But perhaps the lemon was my delirious imagination, which threw up explosions of light and flesh and mangled the features of all my friends—even Arnold's, even Nan's—who were closest to me. We are malleable to a point, then we shatter. Another degree of fever and I would have seen the end of the world and prophesied like the Evangelist; I'm sure my visions were no stranger than his.

As it was, I suffered various manias: a conviction that there were rats in my bed; that water was rising in the flat; that something precious had been stolen from me. In the grip of these convictions, I several times crawled out of bed, drunk with fever and falling with weakness, to search for some bizarre valuable until poor Nan could catch me.

One afternoon, I was tracing with her help my well-worn path from the WC when I returned to myself—an excellent development, yet, deprived of the wings of fever, I could scarcely walk.

"You must sleep," said Nan, and I did.

The next morning I got up, ravenous. Nan had somehow foraged an egg, which she presented like a king on his throne in a little white egg cup. I took off his head and ate every bit and felt no distress. I was cured, the sun was out; life was wonderful. Nan made toast under the grill, which we ate with the tiniest smear of jam, and I wouldn't have traded it for breakfast at the Savoy. By evening, I felt so well that nothing would do but a quick visit to Arnold. Nan was anxious, but I promised not to stay his whole shift. In a lull in the evening raids, I grabbed my jacket—clean and dry thanks to Nan—and set out for the old church.

I didn't get very far before I realized my folly. Though I'd felt fine sitting reading to Nan, once I was on my feet and half a dozen blocks away, I realized that my muscles were jelly and my head full of air. Unwilling to admit defeat, I stopped for a little pick-me-up at a smoky, crowded pub, loud with the false but defiant Blitz cheer and serving very poor lager. As I leaned on the bar to get my breath back, the lights swayed and the floor vibrated with the shock of a nearby mine. Might as well die climbing the tower of the old church, I thought, and I was preparing to leave when I saw Connie disappear behind the blackout curtain. It was him, I was sure it was, even though his bleached hair was now short, and, in an excess of wartime austerity, he was wearing a leather jacket instead of his favorite silk blouse. I pressed through the crush and out the door after him. An intense white and lavender light to the east—that was the earthshaking mine. Dark to the west and—was that a figure already distant on the sidewalk?

"Connie!" I shouted, but weakness and smoke had reduced my voice to a croak. If he heard me at all, he didn't stop; darkness took him so quickly I knew I would never catch up. But he was in London; that was something—if it really was him: the short hair, the leather jacket were against the proposition. On a little consideration, I was inclined to put the image down to residual delirium, and I'd almost discounted the sighting by the time I made my way to the old church. I climbed the steeple and spent several hours watching the fireworks with Arnold, then, at his urging, set off for home early. Buoyed by a very decent sandwich—Arnold's post always seemed well provisioned—I walked home through the fires and damage, evaded one of my warden friends, and reached the flat in good time. The door was open. Raid nearby and Nan in the basement, God bless her. But then I realized that the all-clear had sounded when I'd still been several blocks away. "Nan!"

No answer.

I ran out to the basement steps. "Nan, Nan!"

A sound below. My heart banged into my stomach and both clenched up like a fist. She was lying dazed on the bottom step. I carried her up the stair to the flat.

"It's nothing," she said. "Nothing. I twisted my ankle, that's all."

But as I was putting a blanket around her shoulders, she screamed. I had to cut the sweater away to examine her arm.

"You can mend your sweater," I said to her protests. "Damn, Nan, I think there's a bone broken. I'm sure it's broken."

She didn't want to admit this, and when she did, she was of a mind to walk to the phone box, herself, for the ambulance. "Not on your life," I said, and ran down to call in the report. A broken arm did not sound too bad to the post; she'd have a long wait—and exasperated, I said, "She's nearly seventy. She may have other injuries."

"We have priorities, you know."

That was Liam. It had to be. A damn stickler for regulations. "For God's sake, Liam, I know it's you."

"Francis?" There was something in his voice, some more than casual interest that I registered only too late.

"Yes, of course it's Francis. And she needs help now." I spelled her name for the third time and hung up.

When I got back to the flat, I knew I'd done the right thing, because I saw that her face was bruised too. She maintained that she'd tumbled in the darkness. "You know my sight, dear boy."

I did, and I knew that she maneuvered in the blackout better than any sighted person. She knew every inch of the flat and the basement, too. After I pointed this out, she reluctantly admitted that she'd been knocked over by someone rushing up the stairs. Her sense of a presence in the dark basement had not been illusionary. She would have to go to Bella's, and I would have to keep watch.

Morning dawned before the ambulance came. We rode together to the hospital, the ambulance jouncing over ruts and debris, Nan gripping my hand against the pain. She was for getting the arm splinted and heading straight home. With the ward crowded, the doctor was tempted to let her go, but I complained so loudly that she was assigned a bed.

While they worked on casting her arm, I called Bella to ask about Nan's staying a few days in Holland Park Road. I'd run through my pocket change before I satisfied all Bella's questions and made sufficient explanation for my absence. There I stood in the hall—Nan hurt and my own future cloudy—listening to Bella's laments about the stalled painting and Madame's desires for a color just one (or maybe two) shades darker than café au lait. Truly life begins in tragedy but ends in farce, with some omnipotent prankster hostile even to our dignity. In this case, the crowning touch was a twenty-five-foot ladder, "almost as good as scaffolding," which Bella had obtained. I promised to take a look—anything to get Nan a safe berth.

"All this was unnecessary, dear boy," she said when the ward sisters had her settled at last. "And the expense!"

"We'll think of something." I patted my jacket pockets hoping for a stray pound, and touched paper. The envelope. I must have found it in my delirium and stuck it in my pocket. No matter, I'd hide the photos as soon as I got home.

"What is it, dear boy?" Nan's sense of something amiss is uncanny.

"I've just found those photos in my pocket," I said, and it's a good thing I didn't say more, because at that moment, a heavy figure in a dark topcoat appeared at the end of the ward: my inspector.

Not to put too fine a point on it, he'd come to arrest me. Liam, my former colleague and unregenerate squealer, had called the police as soon as he dispatched the ambulance. I didn't fancy being in the inspector's hands, especially not carrying photos of his recreational pursuits. I might believe (and quite logically) that George Frahm was more likely Damien's killer, but I wasn't willing to rule out the inspector. Not to that extent.

I tried a bluff first. Nan had been injured by someone skulking in the basement. How good of him to investigate. This was a real crime, a real injury, but an old lady with a broken arm was not enough to distract him. I was to be charged, among other things, with evading arrest.

Nan had a few choice things to say about that. I calmed her down, told her not to worry, and leaned over to kiss her good-bye.

She knew what was what. Under cover of my embrace, my light-fingered nanny slipped the envelope from my pocket and slid it beneath the sheets.

"Dear boy," she said, "leave everything to me."

Another of my inspector's acolytes appeared with handcuffs. This one was young and blond and, if anything, even more attractive than Handsome who'd visited our flat.

"You do have an eye," I said, and winked. I nearly wound up at the bottom of the stair for my pains. Remember, Francis, the inspector has no sense of humor!

We got into his big, dark car with the fetching assistant driving for a circuitous journey through the previous night's bomb damage. The inspector remained silent and serious, as befitting a guardian of the law, though at one point he half turned to say, "You've made a serious mistake."

I shrugged. Nan would call Arnold, and Arnold would call a lawyer and then we'd see. I expected my interview to begin promptly, but when we finally reached the station, I was put into a holding cell still populated by the night's catch of the drunk and disorderly. As their numbers thinned out I claimed a stretch of bench and fell asleep, only to awake, stiff and disoriented, by a great rattling at the door. The clock over the desk indicated late afternoon; Arnold had worked his magic; I was getting out.

Or so I thought. Instead, I was marched down the hall to one of the narrow interview rooms. The badly painted stone walls, the stale smoke, the single dangling bulb over the scarred deal table were all familiar. I'd been here before, and the image had lingered in my nightmares. Sitting in one of the two straight chairs was my inspector. With a nod from him, the sergeant took off my handcuffs and left the room. We were set for having a private conversation. Was that good or bad?

I was left to wonder, because he sat and stared at me for the longest time, his heavy brows shadowing his eyes, his jutting nose and strong chin catching the light. His silence and scrutiny were meant to intimidate me, and they were impressive, but he wasn't used to painters. I sat and stared back; he was my type, my original type, before I met Arnold and embarked on civilized pleasure. I thought a ground of Venetian red—there was a purple undertone to the shadows—then maybe cad yellow medium if the picture tended hot, or yellow ochre if it ran cold. Hard to say which would be better; my inspector was a violent man who mostly had himself under control. Mostly, though as I sat there facing a variety of dangers, I realized that what I considered control might be a kind of torpor, such as I had noticed in him before—a suspension of emotion and action until a suitable trigger presented itself. That was not a pleasant thought.

"I am set to charge you with murder, although we might negotiate to manslaughter. That's up to you; I'd expect a confession for that."

This was as fantastic as some radio drama. "You have great expectations," I said.

"You lack an alibi for the murders of First Lieutenant Morris Batchelder and Jeremy Gowen. Whose corpses you conveniently 'discovered'. You have also been pursuing Colin Williams and Aubrey Teck."

"On your orders!" I said indignantly, but I began to fear he might believe all this nonsense.

"It appears," he continued, fixing me with his glacial eye, "that you wish to eliminate anyone who might know of your involvement with Damien Hiller's murder. We know you were acquainted, we know your tastes, we know that on the night Hiller was killed you were in the area where the body was discovered. You won't deny that."

I needed to bring him back to reality. "You were probably in the park as well."

"Pursuant to police duties," he replied.

"Sure. Entrapment and threatening and what's the proper term for fucking in the park?"

He leaned over and struck me in the face. I hoped Arnold would hurry up with a lawyer.

"If you believe all that, why did you coerce me into getting to know Teck?"

"Coercion? You have no proof of that. I don't believe there's any record of that, not a line. And who will be believed? A senior police inspector or a decorator known to half the poofs in London?"

"Strictly Mayfair!" I protested. I wouldn't have him insulting Nan's judgment.

"This is no joking matter. Hiller's death is my priority at the moment." I couldn't help looking surprised at this. And hopeful, too. The RAF man had been the big focus only weeks before. Either they had someone for that, or something else had taken me out of the picture.

"What about our brave boys in blue? Have we stopped losing pilots? Are the Jerries dropping flowers now?"

"A confession in Damien's death," the inspector continued implacably, "is your best bet for your own personal safety. A crime of passion, a lovers' quarrel—I can guarantee you'll escape the gallows."

"Thank you very much, but an innocent man expects to avoid jail as well."

"I don't think you appreciate your situation. You're safe here. And, of course, if you confess, you will remain confined and protected. Consider what might happen if you should be out even on bail. Damien had"—here he had the grace to hesitate—"friends. Friends who might be interested in settling up the score."

"I'll take my chances with Damien's friends," I said, though my recent experiences in Stepney indicated my position would be precarious. But danger is the spice of life, eh, Francis?

"We'll see about that. I expect one of them is in the holding cell by this time. Call me when you change your mind." He opened the door and shouted for the sergeant, who led me back to the cell. It was empty now except for a vaguely familiar figure monopolizing the bench with his feet up and a cigarette in hand, as nonchalant as if he were on a bar stool somewhere deep in Stepney. The inspector hadn't been kidding—or maybe he had a sense of humor after all, because when the guard closed the door behind me, I saw that I was confined with George Frahm.

I felt like a small boy left alone on the playground with the school bully, and, for the first time, I was frightened. Night was coming; the guard might slumber; something disagreeable, even fatal, could easily ensue. It wouldn't be the first time a prisoner had been seriously injured, and I suspected George had been arrested for just that purpose. Here was proof, if any more was needed, how deeply the inspector was involved.

George blew a smoke ring in my direction and settled himself more comfortably on the bench. I'd be damned if I'd sit on the filthy floor—and asking him to shift was clearly out of the question. I leaned against the wall beyond his reach, crossed my arms, and tried to look indifferent. Surely Nan would have gotten in touch with Arnold by this time, and Arnold would have contacted a lawyer. And any lawyer would see that the inspector's case was tissue thin, that he'd been counting on George to frighten me into a confession to poor Damien's murder.

Even under the worst circumstances, such a confession would surely be thrown out, wouldn't it? I didn't like to imagine otherwise. But even temporarily, the inspector wanted a suspect, a confession, everything official. Why was that? Could he know about the photos? I doubted that. He'd only be trading my knowledge for an obligation to George—hardly a rational bargain. But whatever we think, man is no more rational than other creatures; self-interest rules us all, including

George, who was now staring back at me and preparing—I could see clearly how his mind worked—to provoke me in some way.

I would have to attempt charm as a delaying tactic until Arnold could get me out. But not too much. If George did me any damage, I guessed his excuse would be that I had "interfered," as they liked to put it, with him. I shifted my shoulders and positioned myself so that I could keep one eye on George and, with a tilt of my head, one on the duty sergeant, who was doing some paperwork with what struck me as unhealthy absorption.

"Getting tired, are you?" asked George.

"Not a bit," I said, though, in truth, I was beginning to feel wobbly again.

"Might as well make yourself comfortable," he said. "Seeing we're to be mates. You can sit on the bucket."

He was like a great schoolboy. I would refuse to go anywhere near the pestilent-smelling latrine bucket. He would attempt to force me, an assault that he would pass off as innocent horseplay. Where was the lawyer? Nan would not have waited to call, and Arnold must have found a lawyer by this time, must have. And then from somewhere beyond the oblivion of fever, I remembered that Arnold had planned to visit his son at Eton. Could this have been the evil day? Could he have gone early? Taken the boy to lunch, lingered to see the house rugby or a little of the Wall game? Wasn't that what good parents did—not that I'd know about that. "I'd have to turn it over on your shoes."

This touch of levity did not find favor.

He got up, slowly. Types like George savor the moment, but I had no doubt he'd strike quickly enough. He glanced into the foyer where the sergeant was still at the desk, poring over his papers. I smiled to show that I knew what he was up to, that he wasn't going to spook me so easily.

He went to the corner of the cell and shouted, "Are we to have dinner? We're perishing here!"

The sergeant lifted his head, checked the clock over the door, then stood up. It was like watching a play, with every move choreographed. "They're late. I'll check," he said and rose from the desk. George and I stood watching each other until we heard the foyer door open and close, then he lunged at me, and I kicked him with all my strength. He hopped on one foot and swung at my mouth. Instant pain, instant blood. I flailed at his head, connecting with his nose, but he had me caught against the bars of the cell where, being smaller and lighter, I was likely to suffer the worst of the struggle. He gripped my hair for a moment, then decided he'd try to throw me to the floor and shifted his grip. Remembering street fights in France, I lifted my head and snapped it into the center of his chest.

He gave a gasp and staggered back. I picked up the dripping bucket as a weapon and shouted for the guard.

CHAPTER FIFTEEN

I'd like to say I emerged victorious from the fracas—more accurately, I confess a draw. I lost a tooth and collected a black eye; George got a bloody nose, a charley horse where I kicked him, and, as it turned out, the worst of the latrine bucket—a small triumph I intend to savor.

Of course, the duty officer came back in high dudgeon, called for assistance, and made a great show of "securing" the lockup. I admired George's display of righteous indignation and offended innocence, but I knew I'd made a dangerous enemy. Before I saw fit to defend myself, the job had been a business matter; now it was personal, or, as he put it, "I'll have your liver for a fry-up." I wouldn't have put it past him.

Perhaps this comment persuaded officialdom to separate us. George was left in the lockup while I was moved to a smaller cell, from which, very late, I was summoned, still dirty and supperless.

Once again, the interview room. Or one of them. I found the

rooms along the corridor, identical and facing mirror images of themselves, an unsettling touch. This one opened with the usual dungeon rattle and clank to reveal the inspector sitting with an ashtray in front of him. Set to poison my lungs and bring on an asthma attack? Oh, no. The sergeant left, the door closed, and without a word, the inspector drew a photo from his jacket, turned it briefly so that I could see it was a recognizable image of a heavy man without his tweed coat—or his tweed trousers, either—being serviced by a slight, naked boy. He dropped it into the ashtray and struck a match. We sat and watched the paper curl and brown, the images writhing and blackening; under better circumstances I'd doubtless have been inspired.

When it was reduced to ash, my theatrical inspector poked the soft black flakes with one finger. "That's it," he said. "The last of them. You needn't have hoped for anything from those. You have nothing to bargain with. Be assured of that."

I admit to momentary doubt. Could he have seen Nan take the photos? If he had, he wouldn't have hesitated—

"I think now you'll agree that you'll be safest in police custody," he said, eager to clinch the deal.

"I've just been injured in police custody."

"Nothing like what could have happened to you outside."

I wasn't so sure of that: outside, I'd have wit enough to keep well clear of George. As the inspector continued in this vein, I was not so sure he had the rest of the pictures, either. Nan would have offered him one as proof, but I thought I could count on her to keep the rest well hidden. And the inspector hadn't mentioned the strip of film, so clever Nan had kept that, at least, from him. If I had to choose between trusting my Inspector or my old nanny, there was no contest. I'd go with Nan and gamble; I just had to keep my nerve.

"So you have all the photos?" Try to remain expressionless, Francis.

"Of course."

"Which you've already burned."

"No point in having material like that lying around."

"Must have been quite a conflagration."

Was there just a hint of hesitation? I was right, I was sure I was.

"We'll start from the beginning," he said, unscrewing his pen and preparing to write. "Exactly where were you on the night of Damien Hiller's murder?"

I leaned back and folded my arms. "You're lying to me. You don't have all the photos, not all of them. I know you don't."

"The old lady gave them to me," he insisted.

"No, Nan did not. She would not have. I won't believe that unless she tells me herself."

"You want Jessie Lightfoot brought to the station?"

Actually, I didn't want that, but was it inevitable? And if so, where could she leave the photos? Bella's? I saw difficulties there and worse if she returned home, for while the inspector might hesitate about Holland Park Road, he would have no scruples about searching the flat.

"You don't think I'd get them from her?" he demanded.

"I didn't say you couldn't, I said you didn't, because you don't know all that was in the envelope."

He gave himself away then, just for an instant, a little nervous flicker in his eyes, succeeded by something else, a kind of stillness that I recognized as dangerous. For a moment he looked again like the man in the park, the man who got out from behind his desk and his paperwork to enjoy the night.

"You didn't know all they were up to, did you? Not at first. Well, you've discovered for yourself: fun and games with a side of blackmail. The operation was surprisingly ambitious—and under Blitz conditions! It's that 'London can take it' spirit that makes you proud to be English."

He was tempted to strike me, and I caught myself. As with any gamble, I found it easy to be carried away by the thrill of the game. "The films are really impressive—and their filing system too. You should ask George about that."

"You'll be seeing George again if you're not cooperative," he said, but his face had taken on a sallow tone and his voice was hollow.

"I'd stay clear of George if I were you. I'm a gentleman, but George! If he had evidence, who knows what he might ask you to do—dispose of a body and pervert the course of justice, maybe?"

He said nothing, lost in the torpor I had previously observed.

"Perhaps we could come to an agreement," I suggested.

I took his silence as possibility if not assent. "You're safe enough as long as the pictures are with Nan—so long as nothing happens to me. Or to her. Remember that. I'm all for honor among gentlemen of the night, but she would go straight to the press. We have friends at the *Telegraph*," I added. "Remember that, and call off George."

Still silence.

"I took everything," I said, dropping my voice to a whisper. "Your whole file. George doesn't have anything on you now."

We stared at each other so long that his features are locked in my memory. I find them emerging unexpectedly on the faces of my subjects, as if attracted to the violent images that are my forte. Then he put down his pen and folded his hands; he had come to a decision.

"I want those pictures."

"That's understood. When you make arrests for Damien's death and the others, I'll be happy to give them to you. The film, too."

We argued about this for some time, but at last he agreed: I was in the clear after "helping the police with their inquiries." I was free to go, to rejoin my ARP post—he seemed surprised I wanted that, but I knew there was safety in numbers and simplicity in hiding in plain sight—and to return to my easel and to Arnold.

"Very well," he said. "The door's open."

I knew then I couldn't trust him. I saw myself out in the darkness with George perhaps released at the same time—no, no, anxious as I was to leave, I must be patient. "You can have me taken back in the morning. I want my neighbors to know I've been cleared. You understand as warden I have a certain position in the neighborhood."

That was laying it on a bit thick, but he got my meaning, and in the end I was left to doze in the interview room until dawn when I was driven home in a police car. Francis returns with a halo of innocence if not the odor of sanctity!

I immediately searched the flat and the basement, carrying my canvas pliers as a weapon. Then I ventured out, glancing behind me to make sure there was no lingering police presence, and made my way to Holland Park Road, where the price of my visit with Nan was a close inspection of the twenty-five-foot ladder. Sadly, I had to admit it would do. Madame wanted a deep slate gray for the foyer and Bella had laid in a supply.

My mouth was throbbing and I needed a night's sleep, but any port in a storm. I put on my painter's kit and set to work. Nan kept me company for a bit, and when Bella departed to deal with what seemed to be an ever-increasing list of Madame's concerns, I gave her a brief account of my travails and asked where the photos were.

She pointed to her arm, splinted and cast and supported by a sling. "I borrowed some more gauze from the nurses"—translation: she'd pinched a roll—"and I wrapped them around the cast. Except just the one—in case, you know. A good thing, too, because I couldn't reach Arnold."

"And they're still there!"

"Oh, yes. That inspector sat right next to me and didn't suspect a thing. He pawed through my bedding, the nasty man. But I'm afraid I'll get them wet. We'll perhaps put them with Arnold, dear boy. He'll have a safety-deposit box."

We conferred on this and I was looking about for a knife to cut the gauze when Bella came in, postponing the transfer of the photos. "Never mind, dear boy," said Nan. "Safe enough."

At dusk with the sound of sirens and planes already in the air, I put on my warden's togs and rejoined my post. Questions there, as you can imagine. My hasty exit ahead of the inspector had provided them with many delightful speculations. "Police business," I said mysteriously. "You just never know what you're going to run into—or what you'll be asked to do."

Liam, skeptic that he was, would have liked more details. "Mum's the word," I said. Whatever did we do before these so-useful wartime phrases? I'd been replaced, however, on the switchboard; so, asthma and all, I'd be out on call, which is how I labored for the next few nights and was perhaps what saved my life, because I was too exhausted with the smoke in my lungs to do more than return to sleep in the early mornings.

In fact, I was so busy that I almost forgot how precarious my situation was or how little I knew. I hadn't been back to Soho since the night Maribelle hid me; I'd never located Connie, unless that brief, almost ghostly sighting in the pub counted. The inspector wasn't exactly knowledgeable either. His attempt to arrest me for Damien's murder suggested he had no suspects and no evidence whatsoever or, more sinister, that he knew very well who the real killer was and was protecting him. I didn't know which was true, though I suspected the latter. As for the other murders, if the inspector had any evidence, it couldn't be worth much, for nothing seemed to have come of those investigations.

I checked with Nan about that, just to make sure. "Not a line, dear boy," she said.

There it was, and yet the inspector clearly believed that, despite different weapons, location, and type of victim, the killings were all linked. I had that feeling too, and yet I could not have defined my reasons. Perhaps like everyone else I was just too tired. Work days and duty nights didn't leave much time for anything but a few hours of oblivion, and the losses, the deaths, the mutilations of the Blitz—which I was now witnessing nightly—tended to put even sensational private violence in the shade. I might have decided that I really was in the clear and become careless but for an unsettling incident about a week after I'd gotten home.

The foyer at Holland Park Road was finished and looked like the bowels of a battleship. The twenty-five-foot ladder stood waiting to be returned, money from Madame was safe in my pocket, and we had a wet night with near-zero visibility and light raids, what one thought of now as a fine opportunity for an outing. A chance of a lift decided me. I volunteered to take some reports and supplies to a post near Soho. We zipped through the night, wheeling around bomb craters, bouncing over rubble, stopping now and again to commiserate with firemen or fellow wardens or demolition workers. As soon as I made my report, I set off on foot in the mist and drizzle in hopes the Europa was still open.

I was on a little street carved out of the rubble and parallel to Wardour, navigating by a newly issued torch, the occasional smoldering fire, and the lights of the fire trucks, when I heard an eerie tapping behind me. Blind Pew's staff and other schoolboy tales fluttered in memory before the sound resolved itself into a woman moving swiftly in high-heeled shoes. I glanced behind, but the mix of fog and smoke was so thick I couldn't make out anyone nearby.

Of course, sound seems to travel farther on such nights, distorting one's sense of space. Just the same, the footsteps struck me as oddly sinister with a heavier tread than I'd have expected, and there was something forceful, even violent, in that tap-tapping. The very idea of high heels was odd on such a night. The women volunteers would be in gumboots or some sensible footgear; the ladies of the night would hardly be patrolling such an unprofitable, bomb-racked stretch. I didn't like it. In normal life, I'd have ignored the sound or turned and shouted a hello. But this wasn't normal life. Here instinct ruled, and though I was ready to accuse myself of cowardice, I switched off my torch and stepped into what had been a doorway and was now an improvised alley. I felt my way along the wall, listening closely. The staccato tread continued several steps more, then I heard hesitation, a sudden silence on the pavement. I edged farther into the alley, glancing back, expecting a light. None. Silence, then the tap again, but in retreat this time. I waited a moment more, feeling oddly sheepish; I'd let nerves get the better of me. Then I switched on my torch and went off for a drink.

I put this almost embarrassing incident out of my mind until the next afternoon when I returned to Holland Park Road at Bella's urgent request. The kitchen window had finally been repaired and now the smoke damage could be tackled. Though I was not eager to see what gloom Madame wanted spread on the kitchen walls, I needed, for Nan's sake, to keep in Bella's good graces. I got kitted out again and I'd begun priming the wall behind the stove when Nan came in. Bella had been reading her the paper, and the first thing she said was, "Dear boy, do you know there's been another one?"

"Another one?"

"A man with his throat cut. Last night in Soho. Imagine that."

I could, actually.

"Right off Wardour Street."

I went straight out to get a later edition of the papers, where they had the victim's name—no one known to me—and his age, thirty-six. There was a picture: medium height, medium build, brown hair—though who could tell in the dark? He was a locksmith who was part of a rescue squad, going home after work. In some interior compartment, I saw the dark streets, the gray-and-black plumes of smoke, the hadean glow of half-hidden fires, and heard the tap of a woman's heels. I'd been right to find that sinister. A little voice inside my head whispered that it could have been me, perhaps even should have been me, that I was the intended.

Blitz nerves, I told myself. Nonetheless, I'd read the story over three or four times before I got back to the house, and when I arrived, I questioned Nan again about the night she'd been hurt and about the woman she'd heard searching through our flat. But it was not until I was brushing on the paint—stroke after stroke of white, making a bright, almost luminescent surface—that certain ideas began to coalesce. That sometimes happens when I am painting at the easel, too. Ideas appear, though those are ideas for my picture. This was a picture, all right, but of a very different sort.

Someone had been following me. A woman who didn't sound quite right. Perhaps the woman who had searched our flat? Nan did remember a tapping on the boards overhead, so perhaps she was the presence Nan had sensed in the basement, the presence that had tumbled her onto the stone steps? I thought I knew who that woman was, and where she hid so that the inspector, for all his efforts and contacts and knowledge of the night, had never even considered her. My only question now was what I should—or could—do about that.

CHAPTER SIXTEEN

"I need your help," I told Maribelle for the third or fourth time; I was well down on a bottle of prewar Chablis that she'd unearthed to console me for her refusals.

The grayish light, an equal compound of wintry sun and pulverized stone, lit the room, empty except for us and a pair of drunken painters arguing about Braque's influence on Picasso. As if! On another day I'd have urged Maribelle to chuck them out, but not today, when even art was on the back burner, when she was my best, virtually my only, hope of extricating myself from what anyone could see was a fine pickle.

"I don't know, cunty. Police business is not my style. I have a reputation to uphold."

"He's killing off your clientele," I said. "That's not exactly good for business either."

She considered this while I studied her large, handsome face with the high forehead and black eyes. I hadn't been at the easel for weeks.

Not seriously. I need paint, drink, and excitement the way plants need light, air, and water.

"What makes you think he'll come here, anyway?"

"He wants to kill me," I said. And I thought to myself, Would he were the only one!

She was of the opinion that I could take care of myself and, in lieu of assistance, offered advice I had no intention of taking. But finally, the bottle empty, my eloquence exhausted, and my despair palpable, she agreed to let me know if Connie showed up. Without hesitation, I scrawled a message to him and asked her to pass it on.

Maribelle slipped the paper into her blouse and winked. "Keep your powder dry," she said.

Indeed. Out on the street, John shouted hello and came loping over before I could take evasive action. He had a camera slung around his neck and, as usual, looked frayed and tattered, with the greenish pallor of the true night bird. He asked about his jacket, which was safe in the flat, having been well cleaned by Nan. I relayed this, but he was still not pleased, and he was so upset by the loss of his wretched hat that I had to buy him a drink. More than one, actually.

"Have you seen George around?" I asked. We were leaning against the bar in a bomb-damaged pub—our second of the afternoon. Plaster was sifting down from the ceiling, the door was reinforced with timbers, and there was a charred panel along one wall. I diagnosed blast plus an incendiary: I'd developed an eye for the nuances of destruction.

"George?" John either feigned ignorance or had genuinely forgotten. Either was possible.

"Big, tough, and handsome, all parts in working order?"

"Oh, that George! Spot of bother with the police, I understand."

"Still away?" I asked hopefully.

"Far's I know. Didn't you go looking for him?"

"I found him too—unforgettable. A unique experience."

John had much to say about George, in particular, and unique experiences in general. That's John in the afternoon. While in the morning he can scarcely speak without several fingers of gin, by afternoon he's flying with the world on a string, so to speak, and snapping everything that moves. Me, too. I heard the click of the shutter, saw his smile. "Very nice," he said. "You have a certain world-weary expression. Or is it just the Blitz? Buy us another gin, would you?"

I had little in my pocket by the time I finished entertaining John, but I left Soho lighter of heart, hoping, if not confident, that freed of George's threats, my inspector would see that he was kept inside. I liked that idea very much. What I didn't like was what I discovered when I got home. Key in the door as usual, rattle of the knob, followed by the familiar, cheery call of, "You're home, dear boy!" My heart sank.

"Nan, what are you doing here?"

"Oh, home's best. I do love Bella, but I'm managing fine."

"Fine, you're managing fine!" I almost shouted. "Someone has been lurking around the basement, rummaging through our flat. You've been knocked down, had your arm broken—it could have been your neck! Nan!"

"Dear boy, don't upset yourself."

"I intend to upset myself. How am I going to be out protecting the public if I'm worried about you every minute? You're a selfish old woman!"

"Yes," she said, "but I have the photos. Do you think I could have left them at Bella's? She's a demon for cleaning. Nothing untouched, nothing unturned."

I stamped around the flat for a bit, more to impress her with the seriousness of the whole business than out of real anger. I'd talk her 'round tomorrow and get her to go back, though since Bella drove a hard bargain it would surely mean another coat of paint for the kitchen. "It's way too late to take anything to Arnold today," I told her. "You might have thought of that."

"I did think of it. Anyway, Arnold's fire-watching post is hardly the best place for photos. What I thought, dear boy, was a bit of grease-proof paper, another layer of plaster, and they're safe as long as I am."

"You'd be safe as long as you're at Bella's," I reminded her, but I had to admit, if only to myself, that I'd found living at Holland Park Road with the perfect nanny a bit wearying. And given that chance rules all when sea mines, incendiaries, and explosives of all types are raining from the heavens, even banks and safes were probably no more secure than one old woman. In the end I rooted out some plaster of paris and added another thin layer to Nan's cast.

"The doctor will get a surprise when this is taken off," I said.

Nan laughed.

"It's not too heavy? Try to lift your arm."

"Not much worse. It felt like a lead weight before and feels about the same now."

"About the best we can hope for."

"I'll stay upstairs if there's a raid," she said, conceding the danger now that it was too late to move her.

"Oh right," I said, "so I can worry about your being blown up instead of attacked."

With a show of indignation, I went down to the basement, where I found an old door and three segments of some rusty iron fencing that had missed the scrap-metal drive. I used the door to reinforce the kitchen table, and I wired the fencing around it as some protection from flying debris, forming a crude version of a Morrison shelter. Nan pronounced it excellent; I wasn't so sure.

"Don't worry about me, dear boy," she called as I left for my shift.

As if!

Around midnight Maribelle called our ARP post. Even though it was a light night and all of us sitting around, I heard our head warden say no personal calls were allowed. "Not even his mother!" he said—that's how I knew it must be Maribelle—and I was rebuked for giving out the number. I compounded this offense by taking a break as soon as possible and rambling around the building until I found an unlocked office with a working phone.

Under a green-shaded desk light, I dialed the Europa. The phone rang once, twice. "Maribelle?"

"That you, cunty? What sort of place are they running? I nearly gave that stiff-necked prick what-for."

"Sorry about that. We're strictly business here."

"He was in. I didn't recognize him at first, set to chuck him out, I was. 'No ladies here,' I said."

I didn't wait to hear more. "Maribelle, what was he wearing? Was he wearing high heels?"

"Whole kit, dearie. Silk and a little fox wrap. Real silk stockings, too. He's made a fortune on the troops, he has. The room was agog, I can tell you."

"And my note, Maribelle?"

"That's what I'm calling you about. 'From Francis,' I said. He wasn't going to take it. 'Important,' I said, and insisted."

"Did he read it, Maribelle? What did he say?"

"Cunty, he swore a blue streak and tore it up. So I said, 'You'll want to talk to Francis and get things sorted. I expect him tomorrow or the next day. Midafternoon.'"

"Thank you, Maribelle."

"Let me finish—that's why I'm calling. He was as pale as watered beer, with a queer look about him, and not just his makeup, either. He says, 'I'll see about him myself now.' And he left just like that, stamping out on those high heels. I didn't like it, I can tell you."

I didn't like it either, especially when I remembered that Connie and Damien had posed arm in arm one day on the fading green couch in the flat. My guess about our intruder, which I'd half put down to an overactive imagination, was probably correct. And if it was, Nan was in serious danger. "How long ago did he leave?"

"What's it now? Twelve thirty. Maybe an hour, maybe more. We had a real crush at the bar."

An hour, maybe more! A walk to the tube, maybe a delay for a raid. Catch the train to Chelsea. The walk in the dark to our flat would be slow-going, but he knew the way—now I was sure he did. An hour, an hour and a quarter? Close, it would be close. I took a deep breath, put aside loyalties and scruples, and dialed the inspector. If he was in, fine; if not, I was away to Nan.

I heard someone calling me from the front of the museum, "Break's over, Francis." Down the line, the phone rang unanswered. Hurry, hurry, I thought, my stomach contracting. Then the voice of officialdom in the person of a duty sergeant. Was it the same one who'd conveniently absented himself so that George could give me a thumping? I almost hung up, but this was no time for personal pique. I gave my name and asked for Inspector Mordren. "It's a dire emergency."

I could almost hear him yawning. "The inspector's a busy man. You'll need to give me some idea what this is about, sir."

"Is he in? Tell me at least if he's in! He'll want to talk to me. Tell him it's about the killings in the West End he's investigating. Tell him, 'Damien Hiller.'"

A distinct lack of interest; I felt it even down the wire. What did he or his precious inspector care about Nan? About me? "Tell him the photos are in danger," I added. "Tell him that and see if he won't come to the phone."

"The inspector's busy at the moment," he began.

"He'll have your guts for garters if those photos reach the wrong hands. Just tell him 'photos.' Photos!" I was shouting by this time, and somewhere down the corridor my name was called again.

I felt behind me for the door and flicked the lock—might as well be hanged for a sheep as a lamb, and anyway I'd be out the back window momentarily. But the inspector? Had the pestilent sergeant disconnected? No, still silence on the other end. Then, just as I was about to give up, I heard the familiar voice.

There was no time for details. "Colin Williams," I said. "He's been dressing as a woman for months; he's the 'Miss Cherie' of Brighton fame. I didn't take him seriously when he told me he was going to do something about Damien's death. But he has, I'm sure he has. He's on his way to our flat and Nan's there."

"Are you at your ARP post? Wait for me."

"Nan's alone. I'll meet you there."

I hung up and pushed the desk under the window—I knew the drill by this time. I broke a letter opener between getting the paint unstuck and the sash pried open—what shoddy maintenance!—and hauled myself up onto the sill. As the lamp, letter opener, assorted books, and papers hit the floor behind me, I pitched forward into the night and ran.

Running in darkness, a juvenile pleasure of country-house nights, the long grass just damp with evening, the shouts of my cousins from the gloom of the trees, the rising moon soon to make all clear. And other nights with real danger under the cover of real blackness, Nan hurrying me into the big stone-floored kitchen in the basement and covering the windows while shots rang out overhead and a flaming torch flickered somewhere nearby, provoking her to mutter, "The devils! They'll try to fire the house."

Upstairs, Thomas, one of the stablemen, was at a drawing room window with a rifle; my father with another was at the back. Those were the nights of my childhood: rebels in the garden and a tyrant in the back parlor. Other nights, Berlin nights, better lit than this—watch the stoops and dustbins, Francis—but with many sooty alleys and crooked byways, physical and moral, so that I was running, still running, in flight from both respectability and danger with pursuing footsteps far heavier than my cousins' light tread on the lawn. Night and danger. The garish lights of the Alexanderplatz morphed now into the familiar Blitz sky with its vast range of lovely and terrifying effects. Tonight a smoky pallor shot with pink and orange from distant fires cast just enough glow so that I could keep running, my lungs emptying, a flood of images pouring through my mind and washing around the great central fact: Nan was alone and virtually helpless.

I was a few blocks from our street, wheezing like bagpipes, when Moaning Minnie went off. For an instant I thought the sound was inside me, the inner pressure of fear and extreme effort, but our Teutonic visitors hadn't forgotten us. Searchlights bounced big white disks off the clouds and smoke, the guns started up, and the earth quivered with the roar of engines and ordnance and mines and fires.

A few people on the street. "Take cover, take cover," I yelled automatically, though I was out of cover myself and not intending to seek it, unless my improvised Morrison shelter qualified. And the inspector? Where was he and his handsome driver? Close enough to help? And would he? Running and gasping empties the mind of assumptions. He might think that my death—and Nan's—would be a good thing, a lucky thing. And so it would, until they cut off her cast and peeled away the photos.

Don't think it! "Keep down, dear boy, we'll give them what-for." Was it my imagination or did I remember her with a light hunting rifle? Red light washing the kitchen from the small, high windows. I was to run if there was fire. "To the trees, Francis. They'll not see you in the shadows." "And you, Nan? What about you?" "Don't worry about me."

Not likely! A big gulp of air, legs shuddering, then the familiar silhouette of the roof, the chimney pots, the tracery of the lime tree. Up the steps, key in the door. Inspector, police car nowhere in evidence, just darkness and a kind of silence, noticeable even within the sounds of the raid—odd how the ear discriminates. Nan's, too, for she cried out, "Watch out! Watch out, dear boy!"

In that moment, I realized that the door to the flat was open, that someone was in the shadows with Nan. Then a rushing figure, the gleam of something sharp intersecting with a blow from something white before a stinging down my right arm. I lunged into the flat; behind me someone stumbled against the wall.

"The door, the door!" Nan cried. I slammed it shut and slid the bolt, leaving us in total darkness.

I was afraid to move for a moment with Nan on the floor, moaning. "Nan, are you all right?"

"She didn't hurt me. She had that knife. I hit her with my cast." She gave another soft groan. "I've maybe done my arm again."

I felt my way into the kitchen. Found the matches on the shelf near the stove, took several, and struck one. "I called the police," I said. I found a candle and lit it, then helped Nan under the table. "No chance of an ambulance for a bit."

"She was waiting for you. She said she was one of your ARP colleagues, that there'd been an accident, that you'd been hurt. I opened the door like a fool."

"You said 'she'—are you sure?"

"Dressed as," she said. "I'm sorry, but it happened so fast, dear boy."

I found Nan's store of medicinal whiskey and gave her a drink. The raid was close by this time, and the chances of the inspector getting through were dwindling by the moment when we heard someone in the foyer again. I threw open the door.

"He was here," I said. "He was waiting for me with a knife."

One of the patrolmen helped Nan to the basement and promised an ambulance. I went with the inspector out onto the street, sky white now with exploding bombs and flares and all the screams of hell. Fire sirens in the distance followed the earthshaking thunder overhead, as a building near us exploded into flames.

"The streets are mostly blocked. He can't have gone far," shouted the inspector. He sent an officer to the left. He and I went to the right. Maybe not the best arrangement, but we each wanted to keep an eye on the other. And had he still a hope that I could be eliminated, thus solving a raft of problems? Maybe.

At the first cross-street we heard screams from inside a house that had been stove in on one side by a bomb; debris still hot, pulverized brick hanging in the air, wardens not yet on the scene . . . unless you counted yours truly. We pulled aside some timbers hedgehogged with splinters and lifted off the remains of a window to help a thin, middle-aged woman out. She'd lost half her clothes in the blast and was trembling with shock and shouting over and over that "the old man was at the back." We went in over the rubble, dust coming up in clouds, through what had been the house and the garden and was now some new, chaotic hybrid of brick and earth and thorny bushes.

That's what you did—you'd be working away on one thing when you fell into the trouble of the moment and forgot everything else in some desperate activity.

The body was wedged under the second-story timbers. "They'll need a rescue squad," I said.

Lights behind us. My colleagues. "We need a blanket," I shouted. "Two. One casualty."

"You got here fast," said Peter. Had it been his voice calling me down the corridor?

"I'm detailed to the police," I said. That sounded official. "No one else inside, but you'll need a Heavy Rescue Squad to shift the body." With that, I scrambled after the inspector into the remains of the front yard. A fire engine screamed by and, somewhere near, an incendiary flared blindingly white.

"He could be anywhere," said the inspector.

"He's here," I said without the slightest evidence beyond an overwhelming intuition. "You convinced him that I killed Damien."

"I never even spoke to him."

"You didn't need to. You had me asking questions. In his world that's a bad sign; no one he knows does anything except for money or self-interest."

"That doesn't mean he killed the others."

"No, but I'm betting he did. He has a knife." I touched my arm and felt wetness. "Let's see your torch."

In the light I saw that my warden's uniform had been slashed from shoulder to elbow. If Nan hadn't hit him . . .

"We can get him for assault at the very least," said the inspector. I could not see his expression.

The next cross-street was blocked with firemen pouring water on a burning terrace. "He won't have gotten by this," said the inspector. "North or south?"

"North toward Soho," I guessed.

We retraced our steps to link up with his sergeant, and we were nearing my flat when I heard the tap of high heels. I'm still not sure that I heard them—quite impossible, really, in the din of the raid—but suddenly I stopped. Overhead a shower of white-hot parachute flares blossomed like some infernal flowering tree, and there! I grabbed the inspector's arm, there! A slim woman in a light dress, recklessly walking in the midst of the raid. We started toward her and she ran.

Water, hoses, debris, flying cinders, red-hot bits of wood, paper, fabric, a certain fatal fleshy stench, the Blitz smell of gas and old dust, a conflagration of history that screamed and shrieked until we were half deafened. The road was such a mess underfoot that we slipped and stumbled even though the sky was lit up dramatically orange, red, and white amid the black clouds of smoke. Another block and I looked up. Overhead, silhouetted against the fiery glow, was the vast and sinister chute of a descending mine. I shouted a warning, but Connie, no doubt it was Connie now, ran straight on, and though I tried to stop the inspector, he escaped my grip and lunged forward in pursuit.

"It's already on the ground!" I shouted. "It's going to go off! Stop, stop!" Connie half turned, but he didn't falter. Then I saw that we had him trapped. When the mine blew, the street would be blocked. There would be no way out but back, unless—"No, Connie! There's no time!"

But he sprinted forward—he must have discarded his high heels—and the inspector desperately lumbered after him. I stopped. Mine fuses burned for fifteen seconds before ignition; one counted automatically. I made a frantic sideways leap toward the steps of the nearest building and the shelter of masonry and sandbags as the blast obliterated the world. A ball of white fire tinged with lavender tore up to the heavens; the initial shock wave flung me into the wall of the building and hurled debris around me like so much shrapnel. The sound went on and on, the explosion lasting several seconds that seemed like several minutes, while I clung to the sandbags and was slammed back and forth against the building and the steps by the force of the aftershocks.

Finally, a ringing as if the universe had become a giant bell, a Big Ben of nightmare. I ached all over. My tin hat was gone—I would be rebuked for losing equipment again, which troubled me for a moment, a clear sign of shock. I clawed my way upright with the help of the railing. I was on my feet, which was a good sign, but the world was silent; that was not. I thought for a moment that I might be in some dubious afterlife, that I had been blown right through all my assumptions and the line between the real and the not-real. Then I put my hand to my face and touched blood. The dead don't bleed.

When I staggered around the steps, I saw the crater in the light of a flaming building and the inspector lying on the pavement. He seemed oddly foreshortened before I realized that his legs were gone. And Connie? A shoe and some scraps of silk had been blown into the gutter. He must have been immediately next to the mine when it went off. Doubtless bits of him had blown against me in the shock wave. I filled my lungs as best I could despite this thought and managed to reach the inspector. His eyes were open and although I saw that there was overwhelming damage, he was conscious.

"Why?" I asked.

His lips moved. "It would have happened again," he said.

I understood; either I had some residual hearing or I recognized the shape of the words—I haven't struggled to paint the human mouth for nothing—but I knew what he'd said.

I knelt beside him on the pavement. I had no first-aid kit; even if I had, there was no hope for him. "I'll burn the photos. I have them."

"Where?"

"Nan's cast." I held up my arm and mimed the cast.

His face took on a curious expression that might even have been amusement—the inspector was a man of many parts and many layers. It might even be, as the American poet says, *that if I had known him I would have loved him*. Or maybe not; one's sentiments are elevated at such moments. He started to say something but blood came from his mouth and he was no more. I was still sitting there, smack in the middle of the street, when the first warden responded. “Get the police,” I said. “This is a matter for the police.”

CHAPTER SEVENTEEN

I met him in the park—ironic, that, when everything started there, but my newest copper was oh-so-proper and nothing if not discreet. You can see how I'd come up in the world from dodging local vice cops to my own personal inspector to this superintendent—small, wiry, obviously ex-Army. His thinning hair was gray at the sides, and round wire glasses covered cautious slate-colored eyes above a long nose and a wide, narrow mouth. Arnold had told me that he was very senior and straight in every way. Intelligent and self-contained, this police paragon preferred not to be seen with me in a pub and, naturally, I resisted the station house. The park was the compromise; we walked across the scarred, militarized lawns in the direction of the Serpentine. The foggy morning was made darker by the haze of smoke, and the cold air put a hitch in the superintendent's stride; his left leg had been doubtful, he said, ever since the Somme. He stopped gratefully at an empty bench and motioned me to sit beside him.

Another silence; this time I'd drawn a thoughtful copper. I was assembling quite a collection of the breed. There had been the patrolmen, weary and brusque, who had responded to the bomb site; their sergeant, skeptical on general principles; a new inspector, young, smooth, and ambitious; and now this entirely superior and highly respectable being, a superintendent who wanted to sit with me in the park. I felt myself slipping inexorably into the good-citizen category.

He drew an envelope from the inside pocket of his coat and handed it over. "The letter you requested."

It was unsealed. I unfolded a thin, coarse sheet the color of lavatory paper—even official communiqués were beginning to look shoddy with the shortages—and read that I had provided invaluable and material assistance to the Metropolitan Police. My reinstatement to my ARP post was highly recommended.

"Thank you," I said. "That should do it."

"I should think," he said. We watched some hardy ducks waddling along the edge of the Serpentine and speculated silently on a listing barrage balloon beyond the trees. Finally, he spoke again. "There are still questions."

I nodded. I would have said that there was almost nothing but.

"We have closed down the 'club' that Teck and his friends were running, but we'd like to be sure all the photographic material has been secured. I have reason to believe you were in possession of some pictures."

"Lost in a raid, I'm afraid." That was true in a manner of speaking. Nan had reinjured her arm when she hit Connie, and the damaged cast had to be removed. As a result, I recovered the photos and burned them. I can keep my word as well as any gentleman.

"It would be best if they were." He looked at me very directly.

I nodded and there was another long pause.

"Inspector Mordren leaves a family," he said.

I hadn't known that; another surprising layer to my inspector. Though imagination is my strong point, my mind boggled at the spectacle of a domesticated inspector.

"Under the circumstances—"

"To the best of my knowledge there is nothing."

"Good. The reputation of the force is always a matter of concern. Now, on the night in question . . . "

Though I had already told this story to the patrolmen, to the sergeant, and to various detectives and inspectors, my superintendent wished to hear it fresh. He, like the others, balked at the moment before the blast. "Didn't he see the mine descending?"

"Big as a pillar box, with a chute the size of a marquee? One couldn't miss it! And I was shouting warnings like a maniac. Of course, you know what a raid is like, total noise and chaos. But they both had to know. Connie—Colin Williams—figured he could outrun it, I guess. And if he had, with the street blocked behind him, he'd have gotten clean away. His disguise was blown, but he could disappear, change his name, join the forces. He had some hope."

Even as I spoke, I sensed that I was giving Connie too large a share of reason and forethought. He'd gone beyond all that to reside at some different and remote address where I guessed he'd been ever since Damien was killed. All that happened afterward was the result of a few violent moments between his friend and my inspector.

"And John—Inspector Mordren?"

"He was in pursuit. He wasn't counting," I added.

"Counting?"

"Fifteen seconds for the fuse. We're trained to count; it gets to be automatic—you know you have only so many seconds to take cover."

"Which you did."

"Most certainly. I've seen mines explode. I was lucky I wasn't killed as well. Connie and the inspector had no chance."

"We can say that he died in the line of duty." The superintendent did not sound entirely happy.

"I think so."

Then a second suggestion, which made me think that they had a history, that perhaps the superintendent owed my inspector for some great favor. Injured men who survived the Somme often had such friends. "Perhaps he died heroically?" His words were tentative, as if he were trying on the idea for size.

A hero of a certain sort, I thought, and one not at all to my taste. "What about Damien Hiller? Doesn't his death count?"

"Is there evidence?"

I had to shake my head. Only his words, I thought.

"The line of duty then," the superintendent said briskly. "I think that's as far as we can go."

A bit more than far enough, I thought to myself, for the superintendent's tone left no doubt that Damien's death would ever remain a mystery. But maybe the superintendent's decision was fair. Not many people love the good enough—or hate the bad enough—to put themselves in the way of a sea mine. I'd give my inspector, who had known, and feared, himself, that. *It would have happened again*, he'd believed, and maybe on the best of evidence.

I am a different breed. Life is dark and full of violence, but I can live with that if I can climb out of the dumps to paint and drink and carry on. I like life on the edge, and excitement is waiting for me still and for as long as I can keep ahead of bombs and mines and vice cops, crooked or otherwise, and irrational strangers.

I stood up and shook the superintendent's hand. I was free until dark, when I'd have to report to the ARP post. There was no reason not to continue on to Soho for a drink at Maribelle's, for a meeting with Arnold, for the chance of some adventure. And then soon, very soon, I hoped, I would begin to paint again, and attempt to capture all this mess of lust and blood and mangled flesh, bomb light and shadows, naked boys and the huge brutal shape of my inspector. I'd manage to do it now, I was sure I would.

Quotes in Chapter Six taken from
Louis MacNiece translation of Agamemnon

Cover design by Mauricio Díaz

ISBN 978-1-4532-6099-9

Published in 2012 by MysteriousPress.com/Open Road Integrated Media
180 Varick Street
New York, NY 10014
www.openroadmedia.com

MYSTERIOUSPRESS.COM

Otto Penzler, owner of the Mysterious Bookshop in Manhattan, founded the Mysterious Press in 1975. Penzler quickly became known for his outstanding selection of mystery, crime, and suspense books, both from his imprint and in his store. The imprint was devoted to printing the best books in these genres, using fine paper and top dust-jacket artists, as well as offering many limited, signed editions.

Now the Mysterious Press has gone digital, publishing ebooks through **MysteriousPress.com**.

MysteriousPress.com offers readers essential noir and suspense fiction, hard-boiled crime novels, and the latest thrillers from both debut authors and mystery masters. Discover classics and new voices, all from one legendary source.

OPEN ROAD
INTEGRATED MEDIA

CPSIA information can be obtained at www.ICGtesting.com
Printed in the USA
BVOW071028180912

300686BV00002B/2/P